Also by Carol Baum

Murder on the Mountaintop Leads the Way

Murder at the Art Fair Raises the Stakes

Murder at the Museum Paints a Picture

Murder
at the
Castle Wakes
Up the Dead

A Jessica Shepard
Mystery

Carol Baum

ARCHWAY
PUBLISHING

Archway Publishing books may be ordered through booksellers or by contacting:

Archway Publishing
1663 Liberty Drive
Bloomington, IN 47403
www.archwaypublishing.com
844-669-3957

Because of the dynamic nature of the Internet, any web addresses or
links contained in this book may have changed since publication and
may no longer be valid. The views expressed in this work are solely those
of the author and do not necessarily reflect the views of the publisher,
and the publisher hereby disclaims any responsibility for them.

Any people depicted in stock imagery provided by Getty Images are
models, and such images are being used for illustrative purposes only.
Certain stock imagery © Getty Images.

ISBN: 978-1-6657-0895-1 (sc)
ISBN: 978-1-6657-0896-8 (hc)
ISBN: 978-1-6657-0894-4 (e)

Library of Congress Control Number: 2021913245

Print information available on the last page.

Archway Publishing rev. date: 08/17/2021

For Michael and Dan.

One
The Day Begins in Dalkey

D
r. Jessica Shepard got off the bus and looked around. The scene was quaint with a feeling of timelessness. There were charming shops, restaurants, and cafés. Some of the buildings appeared ancient, others less so. For a moment she felt as though if she just stood still centuries would pass by in retrograde fashion. But she needed to find a taxi, and as none were anywhere to be seen, she first needed to find a local to guide her.

"Excuse me," she said. "Would you please tell me where I may find a taxi?" Jessica asked the young man dressed in a crinkled T-shirt, soccer shorts, and cleats. He was heading into a coffee shop nestled in a row of low-lying buildings that ran the length of the street. Jessica had just left the bus that brought her from the Dublin Airport and dropped her in the center of town. She was unsure how close Castle Ryan was to this center of Dalkey, and of the town she knew only that it was a popular coastal Irish village, to which she had traveled southeast from the capital of Dublin.

The man turned from the glass door and flashed a brilliant smile. "Now where would you be wanting to go?" he said.

Jessica returned his smile. "I'm expected at Castle Ryan."

"Castle Ryan, are you? Well, I see. Look, if you are willing to come inside for just a minute while I change my shoes and get myself some coffee, I'll be happy to run you up there myself. It isn't far, and you'll have to wait as long for the taxi to get here. My car's just around the back of the shop. And I'll even treat you to a cup of your own while you wait. I'm sure you'd do the same for me if the shoe was on the other foot. Looks like this is your first time here."

"Oh, I couldn't put you to so much trouble. If you'll just—"

"Nonsense. I'm happy to help a lost American."

"It's so obvious, is it?"

"That it is! But don't feel bad about it. I've got relatives in the States, so I can recognize one of you. Also, I've got a good sense for spotting lost creatures." He flashed another smile, and his teeth revealed a few flecks of dust caked onto them, which he likely obtained in the vigorous game of soccer he had obviously just engaged in.

He graciously opened the door wide, and they went inside. The shop was small with wide plank floors. But the sheen on the floor and the sparkling cleanness of the coffee counter in the back spoke volumes. It was well tended by whoever owned it.

Jessica dragged the small rolling suitcase that had served her well throughout many recent trips to other locales. It was the same one that had traveled to Montreal, Miami, and most recently Paris. All those trips had necessitated the use of Jessica's analytical mind to solve mysteries she never would have guessed would end up involving her. Now her rescuer deposited her at a small table to one side of the shop, to the delight of the few local inhabitants already installed there. It seemed that nothing much had happened yet that morning. And the sight of a new arrival, picked up by the young man in the soccer attire, was providing the needed conversation topic for the rest of the day. They threw her curious glances as she sat down. This particular coffee shop clearly wasn't one that foreign visitors tended to frequent.

There was a young woman tending two large coffee urns at the very back of the shop. She had blonde hair that was so pale it was almost white—except at the ends where hot-pink frosting was growing out. Jessica could see that there was a rapport between the soccer player and this woman by the look they tossed between them.

"Sean, have you taken to picking up stray tourists as a new profession?" she asked playfully and loudly enough so her comment was heard throughout the shop and received its expected chortle of amusement from her few grateful audience members.

"Now Millie, don't be rude. I'd expect better of you. You'll be making our American guest here think we're not hospitable. Two cups of coffee, please, with everything on the side." He leaned his muscular elbows on the counter and said loudly and archly, "She's heading up to Castle Ryan. I wonder what's waiting for her there."

All heads turned toward him, and for just a moment, Millie paled to a shade even lighter than the hairs on the top of her head. But even from the distance of her table in the corner, Jessica saw the woman's blue eyes twinkle with amusement a few seconds later.

"Now Sean, is that a fact? And please get your sweaty elbows off my clean counter! I've just finished wiping it down and I don't need you to dirty it up!" She took out a cloth and proceeded to wipe the surface vigorously until she was satisfied it had met her high standards.

Sean turned back to Jessica and asked, although she was sure he didn't need to, "Didn't you say you wanted to get up to Castle Ryan? I heard you correctly, didn't I?"

Jessica began to feel something between irritation and dismay at the time it was taking for her to be on her way. She got up from her seat and went over to join them. "Is there a problem? I'd be happy to call a taxi if you have a number I could call. I really think I should best be going."

"No. No. You don't need to do that. I've told you I want to drive you up there," Sean said. "I'm happy to do it. It's just that there's a local legend about the castle that foreigners don't usually know about and only silly locals, like Millie here, believe in. I'm just giving her a little ribbing about it. She doesn't mind. Millie and I go way back, don't we, Millie? We've always had good times together, haven't we?"

"I'm not silly!" Milly said. She harrumphed with a force to match any opposing member in either of the Irish legislative houses. And she slammed down the palm of her hand on the counter, totally forgetting the prior exhortation she had just directed to her friend. She threw her gaze directly at Jessica and enunciated each word with exaggerated precision. "My grandmother told me about it many times, and she doesn't make up stories, although she certainly likes to tell them to anyone who will listen to them with respect. That much I'll admit to even you, Sean! But she's a very practical woman just like me."

She gave a confident jerk of her head and then turned away from Jessica and Sean, adding, "And let me make it very clear that I've no intention of taking any more ribbing from you, Sean Telford."

Sean meekly truckled and picked up the tray on which Millie had placed two mugs of coffee, only half-filled and with no sugar or cream beside them. Some of what little coffee had been poured into the mugs splashed over the edges of the bone china and wet the surface of the tray. He went behind the counter and grabbed cups of sugar and cream and added them to the tray. He nodded sideways to Jessica and led her back to the table where he had originally left her.

By this time, the two elderly women, who were sitting immobile at the neighboring table with their own pots of tea between them, had their eyes permanently glued on Jessica. It was obvious that for them the gratuitous show was getting better and better, and their seats were in perfect position to observe all the scenes.

"Don't mind me. No one else but Millie does," Sean said once he and Jessica were seated. "You can see that I just like to get a rise out of Millie. But in my defense, she's such an easy target." He laughed, and Jessica felt the pleasant sensation of camaraderie flowing through her. She decided to put off her usual habit of getting to a destination without any unnecessary delay and decided she would spend the time necessary to probe her new acquaintance, at least for a bit.

"So tell me: why all the mystery about the castle? No one mentioned anything about it to me. I just assumed it was a luxurious inn. I didn't suspect there was anything else to it."

"There's not really that much of a mystery."

"But obviously from your conversation, there is."

"Well, I said foreigners don't usually know about the castle's history. But since you ask, they say"—he put up two fingers of each hand as if in quotations to accentuate his introductory phrase—"a local woman married the very rich man who built it for her many years ago. Supposedly she turned out to be an independent sort, especially for that time, and liked to write stories and such. Well, *her story* goes that at first her husband indulged her creativity, like it reflected back on him or something. She used to read her stories to family and guests who visited. Presumably her husband thought she'd take it no further than that—or at least publish under a man's name. But when she decided to publish under her own, the story goes that there was a big blowup between those two. Then she ended up *dead.*"

"Oh no!"

"Oh yes. Apparently, it was never clear if she ended her life or if it was ended for her."

"How horrible! And just think how I didn't know anything at all about it. No wonder Millie's so touchy about it. I guess I would be too, if I lived here."

"Yes, I guess you would be, especially being a woman. You all stick together, don't you? But those were different times. Different times. That's a fact."

"I should say so. And aren't we lucky about that?"

"But don't worry. I told you I just like to tease Millie because she's the kind who's always telling tales behind the counter about this and that story her grandmother told her when she was small. She's inherited that verbal trait from her grandmother. Now don't get the wrong idea. The castle is a very charming inn, just like you thought, and many a tourist—just like yourself—spends a very pleasant stay there."

"Well, that sounds more encouraging."

"Yes. Pretty gardens there are, all about the place wherever you look. An old girlfriend of mine used to like me to take her up there for tea on a Sunday."

"You don't look like the type who would enjoy that."

"I'm not. But she was a *looker* so I went along with it. She used to make me sit with her on their back patio. You can imagine how well that went over! Well, look at *me*. Do I seem like the kind that would go in for that kind of thing? I should say not. *Looker* or not, it didn't last long." He pointed at himself with both his forefingers and once again flashed Jessica an ingratiating smile. By now, the few swigs of coffee he had drunk had washed away any residue of the soccer dirt on his teeth, making his point somewhat less dramatic than it would have been if the traces of dirt had still been there.

He didn't notice Jessica concentrating on his teeth but

continued trying to repair the local hostelry's image and said, "If you like fields of yellow gorse, you'll find plenty of them up there. They've also added an indoor spa since I went for the tea. Still, neither much in my style, but *you'll* probably like the place."

He sized Jessica up again and then said, "The family Ryan does a good job running the castle—the mother and father, and the daughter, Alice, and son, Joel. Joel used to be a fair soccer player, but he's now so busy working up at the castle that we don't see much of him playing anymore. It's a damn pity that is."

He took one more appraisingly shrewd look at her and said, "May I ask, though, why a woman like yourself would be wanting to stay there alone? Or are you meeting up with someone? You don't look to me like the type that would want to while away your hours up at Castle Ryan all by yourself."

Jessica was learning that the local gregariousness was accompanied by a good healthy dose of curiosity. *But what's the harm in opening up to a new acquaintance?* she thought. The reason for her visit would be common knowledge soon enough.

"Well, this may sound a little strange to you, but recently I've found myself in the midst of some unusual occurrences. They have sparked the interest of a producer and a screenwriter who may potentially dramatize them as a television miniseries. You could say that they bribed me with a promise of a vacation in your charming village while we discuss it. They want to use this general location, working in the various plots around my experiences. I'm here to sound out some of their ideas with them."

"That sounds exciting—but mysterious. So I guess Castle Ryan's the right place to do it. What kind of *occurrences* are you talking about?"

Jessica paused for a moment, still unsure how much to relate or if he would believe her. Quickly running them over in her mind, the details of her last three exploits did seem almost too coincidental for anyone to believe, if those on the receiving end were possessed of a realistic nature.

First, there had been her trip to Montreal, where she was forced to deal with the death of her former mentor on the rugged terrain of Mount Royal; then Miami and the loss of an elderly, new friend who happened to identify his family's precious art from pre-World War II Germany; and most recently, there was Paris and the death of a brilliant museum employee amid financial machinations involving the museum, artworks, and a château in the French countryside. How all of these episodes would transfer to the landscape of this Irish coastal town she would hopefully soon learn once she met with Louis Aspen and Michael Thornes.

But for now, all she could wonder was if Sean would think she was just ribbing him, like Millie had accused him of doing to her. But then Jessica looked at Sean's expectant face, cupped in his hand, waiting for her story, and she figured she would risk his skepticism.

So she said, "It seems fate has conspired to turn me into some type of amateur detective of murders. And the men that I'm meeting with think they'd make a good backbone for the television series that they're looking to create."

Rather than skepticism, Jessica saw Sean take in what she had just said, mull it over in his brain, and accept it as fact. He nodded his head slowly, up and down in a slow beating motion like a bungee cord at the end of an amusement park ride, and said, "Well then, Castle Ryan does indeed sound like the perfect place to talk it over with these movers and shakers, doesn't it?"

"I guess it does. I haven't allowed myself to think much farther than getting here and finding out what the bare outline of their ideas is."

"Yes. Castle Ryan. The perfect place. The perfect place. That's what I think." He nodded again. "Look, let me finally change my shoes and get you over there like I promised. You've waited long enough. Let's get you on your way now."

"Thank you. That would be great."

"Are you done with your coffee? If I get you up there quickly, there's probably much grander fare for you. But don't tell Millie that I told you that. Now that would lead to the last time that she'd let me use her place to change my shoes and clothes!"

"Yes, I'm done with it." Jessica looked down at the mug of coffee that she hadn't yet touched. She really had no taste for it after her little tête-à-tête with Sean. But as she didn't want to appear rude and leave a bad impression of American manners upon being greeted so hospitably, she took a quick sip of the now cold brew. The liquid was surprisingly still tasty and bracing, but one sip was enough, and she put the mug back down on the tray with a flourish.

"Good. I'll be right back. It shouldn't take me more than a minute or two. I promise you that. Millie keeps my shoes in the storeroom. Even if I rib her brutally, she doesn't want to not support one of the best players in the local soccer club despite what I just told you before."

He chortled and walked with a proud gait to the counter, and then he disappeared behind a door in back of it and returned in the promised few minutes in a clean T-shirt, jeans, and sturdy brogues. The cleats he had previously worn were hanging by their tied laces from his hand. And his soccer clothes were tumbling out of a paper bag that he had obviously pilfered from Millie's shop's stores in back.

He grabbed Jessica's rolling suitcase. The cleats were now banging against the leather of the case with every bump in the floor due to their new position straddled across the metal handles. And they left the shop while Millie studiously ignored them and the two elderly ladies, for all outside appearances still enjoying their morning tea, watched their every move until the shop door banged behind them, signaling the morning's entertainment was over for the day.

Sean's was a small yellow vehicle, which seemed almost too tiny to comfortably fit his generous frame, let alone also that of Jessica. Yet the car was possessed of a surprisingly capacious trunk; it easily accommodated Jessica's suitcase after he pushed aside some soccer equipment to the recesses of both sides of it.

A few minutes later, Jessica was miraculously squeezed into the left of him as they drove up a long, winding road toward Castle Ryan. The road climbed up steadily from the flatter areas around the central town, and the scenery was pleasant to observe as the car *put-putted* along. Now finally, the fatigue of a trans-Atlantic flight was taking its toll on Jessica, and she thoroughly appreciated Sean's kind gesture of transporting her so graciously up to the castle by this little yellow car, despite the tight quarters.

Hedgerows of green shrubbery dotted the landscape. And the green of the grass and the shrubs was startlingly brilliant. The verdant hue sparkled in places, caught by the sun's glare that broke through the overhead canopy of trees: here a little darker, there a little lighter, but never losing the touch of emerald that tied the landscape together in a single green palate. The gorse that Sean had described was also on full display; its yellow color merged with that of the car but fought valiantly for dominance over the other color with some success. The coarse spiny shrub seemed to be everywhere, even along the hedgerows and most abundant in rough and grassy fields. Its happy brightness smiled at Jessica and defied any trepidation that might have been inspired by Millie's concerns or fatigue from arrival in a foreign country.

The road wound around, higher up in elevation as they

drove farther from the coastline. As the car moved along, Jessica's appreciation for her driver's kind gesture grew with the length of the drive. She began to feel uncomfortable about taking Sean so far out of his way. But then, almost at the point where she felt she should express her concerns, the car slowed down and made a sharp turn into a clearing in the shrubbery.

A sign, off to one side of the road, had large Gothic letters that identified the property as that of Castle Ryan and the proprietors of the property as Bevin and Brenda Ryan.

There was a long, broad, gravel driveway in front of them that led back on a straight path, and at its end stood a Victorian home of generous proportions. It rose up grandly over the surrounding greenery. The building was of red brick, and even from a distance, Jessica was able to discern that the individual bricks had darkened areas around their peripheries, attesting to the age of the building. It had likely stood in this very spot, unaware of the many, many passing years since the local laborers laid brick and mortar upon brick and mortar to create the castle that persisted in its current form.

Coming closer, Jessica saw it was built in the Gothic Revival style, and it blended naturally into the verdant tableau. There was a continuation of the gravel in a semicircle plaza abutting the castle, which formed a large, welcoming expanse in front of the building.

Sean stopped the car on the gravel and got out. She followed suit. He then pulled Jessica's suitcase from the trunk and handed it to her.

"Well, I'll be leaving you here. Have a good stay. And again, don't mind my ribbing. I do it all the time. I consider it part of my charm. I hope you agree with that assessment." He smiled broadly, obviously confident she couldn't agree more with the sentiment.

"Thank you again for taking me up here," Jessica said. "I

hope I haven't taken you too far out of your way and cost too much time out of your day."

"It was no trouble at all. I was glad to do it. And forget about what Millie and I joked about back at her shop. The Ryans are great people. They really are—all four of them. If your experiences do become televised though, be sure and let me know if there's a part in them for me! I think I could handle it. Maybe a murder on the soccer field or in the locker room? It could work, I think."

"I'll do that."

"Good. Well, good day to you. It was grand to meet you."

He smiled again and got back into his yellow car, leaving Jessica to see for herself what Castle Ryan had in store for her.

Two
Castle Ryan
Welcomes Its Guest

Jessica opened the dark, oaken door of Castle Ryan with some effort and pulled her suitcase over the stone saddle on the floor. Looking up, she saw a cavernous entrance hall illuminated by a massive chandelier that was balanced high up in the center of the vaulted and beamed ceiling. After hearing Sean's and Millie's dark stories about the castle, she felt the odd sensation that the chandelier was hanging over her like a sword of Damocles. She scurried beyond its dangling circumference and walked farther into the interior of the castle. Eager to assess the hostelry that Louis Aspen and Michael Thornes had chosen for the discussion of a potential television series, she thought a good look at it would give her a hint of the mood the two men were after.

Past the entrance hall, there was an intricately carved, wooden staircase with a floral motif. It rose up grandly to the second level by a series of sharp turns and landings. It reminded Jessica of the stairs to a railway station as it zigzagged back and forth between the first and second levels. To the side of the staircase was a broad counter made of the same dark, highly polished wood that seemed to make up much of the interior of the inn. Behind the counter, and above the paneled wainscoting of the hall, was green-and-white striped wallpaper with finely drawn renditions of trees and tiny birds who frolicked. It brought the flora and fauna of the surrounding landscape into the Victorian building that had intruded on the secluded natural setting.

The Victorian mood was reinforced by a few pieces of ornate furniture spread about the room. Jessica imagined that at another time, long, satin skirts shuffled across the flagstones of the hall and were carefully arranged into place once the feminine owners of those lush fabrics positioned their graceful forms onto those generous seats. Seeing a circular brass bell on the counter, Jessica walked over to see if it was pressed whether it would summon one of the Ryans to the now empty hall.

"Here goes. Let's give it a try," she said, pushing down hard on the bell.

A sprightly *ping* echoed through the vestibule with surprising force considering the tiny size of the bell and the massive dimension of the castle's entry hall.

Soon a small woman about sixty years of age came out of a closed door behind the counter. The dark-red of her bob was an unmodulated shade, suggesting it came out of a bottle rather than being natural. The color just missed the trick in making her appear younger than she was; it was unable to hide subtle signs of age evident on her face. Jessica, not one to miss minor details, subconsciously cataloged them in her mind with another: the limp the woman had as she approached the counter. She wore a white, linen blouse, which served to further highlight the bright redness of her hair. That she was proprietress of Castle Ryan was confirmed by her greeting. She said politely, "I'm Mrs. Ryan. How may I help you? Are you staying with us?"

"Yes. I am. I'm Dr. Jessica Shepard. Louis Aspen made arrangements for me to stay here. I don't know if he's arrived yet."

"Yes. Yes. Of course. Mr. Louis Aspen, the television producer. He will be arriving soon with another gentleman, Mr. Michael Thornes." Not checking the computer on the counter or the guest book to its side, she pulled the names easily off her tongue. It gave Jessica encouragement that the producer and the screenwriter she was expecting would actually appear and this wasn't a ridiculous scam or joke someone was playing on her. "Mr. Aspen made the arrangements in advance, Dr. Shepard. We have your room all ready and tidy for you."

"Thank you. Then they haven't arrived yet?"

"Oh no. They're coming in tomorrow."

"Tomorrow? Oh, I thought they'd be arriving today."

"I can see you're starting to fret. Now don't worry about anything. Everything's under control. When Mr. Aspen made the arrangements, he said he wanted to give you a day to relax and get settled after your trip. He told me to be sure and take good care of you. We'll make you feel right at home. Don't worry about that."

"Thank you. I'm not."

"And as soon as he arrives tomorrow—he said he's coming at the same time as the other gentleman—I'll let you know. As I said, don't worry." She looked down at her guest book. "Yes, I'm correct about the date and the name of the other gentleman—Michael Thornes."

"Yes. He's a screenwriter. They'll both be staying here while I am."

"Yes, isn't this exciting!" Brenda twittered and continued her new-arrival monologue. "You'll be in the right wing of the castle, and they'll be in the left. But the wings are close enough on the second level that you shouldn't miss each other coming and going. We serve meals in the dining room or in your room if you prefer. And we have a beautiful outdoor patio in the back by our gardens, weather permitting. But this time of year, they're quite beautiful."

"Yes, I heard about them."

"I bet you have. We also have a library that's perfect for quiet conversations, if you'll be wishing to talk privately to Mr. Aspen and Mr. Thornes. We can serve tea, coffee, or stronger drinks in there. And we have a small conference room, and an indoor spa. They're both located on the lower level. By the way, if you haven't brought a bathing suit, we have some for purchase. You're a small thing, aren't you? But I'm sure we have a few in your size. My daughter, Alice, keeps all the women's sizes in stock. She thinks of everything, that girl. But there, that's a proud mother talking about her only daughter."

"That's OK. I don't think I'll be needing a swimsuit. I hadn't planned to swim while I'm here."

"Well, you look like a lady who knows her own mind. I could tell the moment I set eyes on you. Oh, how I'm running on and on. My husband, Bevin, says it's a failing. We've been married long enough that we can tell each other things like that without taking offense. But between us," she leaned forward confidentially and whispered, although no one else was there, "I think it's one of my virtues." She twittered again. "I tell him that's one reason my guests come back. Men just don't understand these things as well as we women. You know that, don't you?" She didn't wait for an answer. "Anyway, come with me. Let's get you settled in your lovely room."

She moved away from the back of the counter and lifted up the part that was supported by brass hinges so that she was able to come out in front of it. Jessica noticed that Brenda Ryan favored her right knee.

"I can see you spying my knee. Since you're a doctor, I don't mind telling you that it is a misery for me. Dr. Matthews—he's my general practitioner. He has an office back in Dalkey, but I doubt you'll be needing his services. Anyway, I've trusted him for years. He says the only way I'm going to stay away from the operating theater is to stay off my feet. But how can I do what he tells me to when I've got this huge inn to run? I can't leave everything to Bevin, Joel—that's my son—and Alice, can I?"

She shook her head to emphasize the impracticality of her doctor's advice. "Don't worry. I don't expect you to say anything against one of your own profession. I know you wouldn't do that. I imagine you're all thick as glue. And that's as it should be, I guess. I'm just speaking my mind. I told you I do that."

"That's quite all right."

"So shall we get you up to your room? I've got a beauty for you. It looks out over the hills in the back and onto the gardens. In the morning when the sun's just coming up, you'll appreciate the view. And then you'll thank me for placing you there. It's so very pretty. You'll see. And once you do, then you'll tell me I was right."

Brenda slowly, but with determination, led her new guest across the entrance hall to a small elevator on the other side of the room. The sight of it made Jessica breathe a sigh of relief because she wasn't eager to lug her suitcase up to the second level of the castle by the staircase. She also couldn't imagine Brenda easily navigating the stairs with her weak right knee.

As the elevator creaked up to the second floor, the proprietress said, "If you do have something to eat on the patio, watch out for some of those birds that swoop down to share our food." She chortled. "There are a few terrors around here, but we manage right enough. I always figure as long as the birds remain, we're doing something right in tending our gardens, aren't we? When they disappear, that's when we know we're not taking care of them as we should. Just remember to keep your napkin over the breadbasket, and you'll be fine. Well. Here we are."

The doors creaked open, and Jessica followed Brenda out onto the landing of the right wing of the castle. The wallpaper on the second level rose above the paneled wainscoting, as it had on the level below; here it was cheerful with a bright-yellow background punctuated with bunches of small, purple pansies. The general effect was welcoming to any new arrival.

But as soon as they turned the corner of the corridor, a large, carved, wooden owl stared back at Jessica from the top of a shiny, black plinth positioned against the wall. The bird's facial features were so lifelike that the unexpected sight of it made her jump, so that she almost lost her footing as she caught the heel of her shoe on the carpeting lining the plank wood flooring. Two large circular eyes on either side of the bird's triangular beak dared her to proceed farther down the corridor.

Brenda laughed heartily and, despite her small stature and demonstrated limp, was sturdy enough to keep Jessica from falling on her face by grabbing her arm and supporting her at just the right moment. "You don't like owls, do you? I can see that. It's clear as day. But don't mind him. He just comes with the territory."

"I do like owls. Actually, I do. I just didn't expect to see one here—and one that looked so serious. I was caught off guard. That's all."

"Joel and Alice—I mentioned my children—they found that silly, old, carved bird in the attic when we were poking around up there some years back. Don't feel bad. We were all just as startled when we found it staring at us like that under some old things in the attic. Never expected to find it up there. But you know how old houses are. You never know what surprises you're going to come upon at one moment or the other, in some corner or the other."

"I guess not."

"Well, they thought this was as good a spot as any for it after they decided they had to bring it down from there. I was against it at first. But I was overruled, even if I am the mother. They said it reminded them of their old maths teacher, so I guess they thought they were being very funny putting it here for the guests to see. Their way of getting back at their teacher for a few bad grades, I would wonder."

"That'll do it, I guess."

"During the holidays, they like to dress up the old bird with different hats, and capes, and other things. Although to tell you the truth, I think that they're getting a little old for those kinds of pranks. Oh well, the exuberance of youth. What else can I say? They both must have inherited their sense of humor from my husband. I'm sure they didn't get it from me."

Brenda opened wide the door to Jessica's room, and they entered a spacious, sunny chamber with a large, four-poster bed covered by a blue, sateen, quilted coverlet. A vanity table and a small writing desk were positioned against the wall, each on either side of a set of large windows.

Jessica went over to the windows and pulled apart their brocade curtains to look outside. Behind the back of Castle Ryan and its generous flagstone patio, she saw a long expanse of grass, which seemed to stretch for at least an acre; it was the color of emeralds, with well-shaped buxwood parterres surrounding beds of roses. Red roses nestled their heads beside those of pink roses in a riot of brilliant color, enhanced by the deep green of the hedges that struggled to contain their fully blossomed buds.

Closer to the back of the castle on the large, slate patio, metal tables and chairs, whose white scrolled backs were fabricated in the design of harps, were strategically positioned so as best to enjoy full views of the gardens. A few guests were sitting at the tables.

Brenda joined Jessica by the window and said, "That's the view and the patio I was telling you about. Do you like the chairs? Aren't they adorable?" She didn't wait for a reply. "I saw one like them in the local antiques shop and had them made special for the inn. The harp is the traditional symbol of Ireland. I'm not sure if you're aware of that, being American as you are. Some say it represents the *immortality of the soul*. Oh well. That's for deeper minds than mine to ponder. I just thought they were pretty. And they're pretty comfortable to sit on if you do go out there for lunch."

She looked down at the carpet under her feet. "My, these carpets soften the floor for my knee. That they do. But I should be getting back downstairs. I'll leave you to get settled. Once you're all stowed away, why don't you go down to the patio and get something to eat? You can try out my chairs and let me know how you like them."

She looked at her wristwatch. "You still have about an hour before lunch is over. Let me know if you need anything." She finally handed Jessica the key to the room and left, closing the door behind her.

Jessica sat down on the edge of the bed, sinking gently into the welcoming softness of the bulky, sateen coverlet, and she took a slow, deep breath. It was the first time she was alone with a moment to think since arriving in Ireland.

When Louis Aspen contacted her with his idea for a television project about her experiences and regaled her with his ideas for its projected success, she thought it was all a big joke; she couldn't hazard a clue as to who was behind it. But she quickly learned the producer was being totally serious.

Jessica had only recently returned from Paris after a much-needed vacation there with Alain Raynaud. *Alain.* Would she ever have thought when she first met the Canadian narcotics inspector in Montreal they would end up in an intimate, although often interrupted, relationship that seemed to be associated with as much emotion as mystery?

After investigating unsavory occurrences at a private art museum in Paris and then unwinding on vacation, she had just been getting used to her quieter life in her home in Connecticut, back in the United States. And Alain was back in Montreal—now with even greater acclaim after yet one more successful murder investigation, which had been solved in good part due to their diligent teamwork in identifying those behind it.

Aspen introduced himself by phone when he first called her, totally expecting Jessica to have heard of him. He exuded all the confidence of the consummate egoist. Of course, she hadn't. But that hadn't deterred him. "Is this Dr. Jessica Shepard?" he asked over the phone.

"Yes. It is. To whom am I speaking, please?"

"I'm Louis Aspen. You've probably heard of me."

"No. I'm sorry. I haven't. At least, not that I can remember."

"Oh." Without a missed beat, he said, "Well, no matter. I'm a producer of highly successful television series. And I'm currently working on some exciting projects in Ireland. I've heard about you, and I'd like to invite you to come over to meet me and one of my screenwriters there. We can talk about the exciting ideas I have once you arrive."

"I really can't imagine why—"

"Now wait a minute. I can hear skepticism creeping into your voice. But you needn't worry. I'm being entirely serious. I've heard about your serendipitous involvement in a few murder investigations—first Montreal, then Miami, and most recently Paris. I think your stories would be excellent fodder for a series I have in mind. No sure yet if I could pull out from them a miniseries or even more than that. I'll have to see how everything plays out."

"But—"

"I think I'm just the man to put the project together in a way you'd be proud of. I like to consider myself somewhat of an auteur." He chuckled over the phone. "So you don't have to worry about getting involved in anything tawdry or *gruesome*. No blood splattering onto ceilings two flights up or across the room, or anything like that. I can tell from your voice you're a *cultured* woman."

"Mr. Aspen, I really have no intention—"

"Louis, please. I don't think there's any need for such *formality*."

"OK. Louis. As I was saying, I haven't even considered writing down anything about what has happened."

"Not a problem. Not a problem at all. I've already thought of that. Do you know Michael Thornes?"

"Michael Thornes? No, I—" Jessica racked her brain to think if she was missing something she shouldn't have.

"Yes. Michael Thornes. He's an excellent screenwriter. I've worked with him a number of times before on various projects. He's a little quiet to talk to, but he does a very good job once he gets pen to paper, or finger to computer—whatever you want to call it. Almost consider him a partner. And he's very interested in coming on board the project with us."

"*Us?*"

"Yes. Now Jessica, just hear me out. *Hear me out.* That's all I'm asking at this point. Let me map out what I've been thinking about. If you just let me do that, I'm sure you'll agree my ideas have great possibility."

Aspen outlined the rough edges of what he had in mind. It was to be at least a five- or six-part series initially, set in Ireland, where he thought he had the best chance of successful backing. He provided no details about finances. But he assured her he was confident that if he met with her in person, she would come totally along with the project.

He tempted her with the persuasiveness of his colorful words and descriptions of the local beauty of the costal Irish village they would stay at while negotiating. Of course, he invited, she should certainly search what she wished to about him for her own reassurance. He was a legitimate producer, he told her.

He had heard of her adventures from her friend, Tom Martine, who was a freelance investigative journalist who had gotten her and Alain involved in their last investigation in Paris. That connection between Tom and him, although not very close, should comfort her when she did her research, he said. He wouldn't expect anything less of her than that she should investigate his background.

She hadn't found anything disturbing about him and ended up taking him up on his offer. She agreed to meet him face-to-face and hear him out. She didn't dare let her mind jump to the obvious next step and anticipate what Alain's reaction would be to all this. That aspect of the plan she would hold in abeyance—at least for the present.

Now here she was with a full day to think over her impulsiveness before Louis Aspen and Michael Thornes arrived at Castle Ryan. "Well. You made your bed, didn't you? And here you are sitting on it." She looked up at the bed hangings that matched those by the windows and covered the bed's massive frame. "Well, at least it's a beautiful four-poster to lie in, if I have to lie in something. I can say that for the place."

But Jessica wasn't tired. She didn't want to lie down, at least not yet. She decided she would take Brenda's suggestion and scout out the patio restaurant to see what other guests might be holed up in this castle with a history.

Three
Tea for One

J essica entered the large dining room and saw a young girl standing behind the hostess stand. One glance at her thick, auburn hair was enough to clinch it had to be Brenda's original shade, which the older woman had hoped to recreate, but without success. A second look at the girl's name tag confirmed her to be Alice, Brenda's daughter. Alice looked up and smiled warmly as Jessica came over.

"Are you lunching now?" Alice asked.

"Yes. I am. I thought I'd try the patio." The dining room was empty. It seemed that whatever guests were currently housed at the castle and partaking of its culinary selections had also decided to enjoy the good weather, and that the patio was the best place to do so.

"My mother told me to expect you to come down soon enough. Is everything all right with your room?"

"Yes."

"It's a nice one you've been given. I like the right wing best.

It's newer than the left wing, you know, so the rooms tend to be sunnier than those on the left. The building's *so old*. Some do prefer the left, but I like the right better." Jessica could see that a good deal of Brenda Ryan's social skills and wordiness had been handed down to her daughter.

"The room's perfect. There's nothing amiss with it. Thank you."

"Fine. So why don't you come with me. I'll take you out to the patio for lunch. There's a few other guests out there now so you won't be sitting all by yourself like a statue in a garden."

Jessica followed Alice through the dining room. It was already set up with white tablecloths and gleaming silverware. The evening meal was sure to be a formal offering from the look of things. Jessica thought that even with the good weather, for the evening meal, guests would happily descend from their rooms to enjoy the elegance around her. But for now, they passed by empty tables on their way to the patio.

Alice opened glass doors that led outside. The outdoor tables Jessica had seen earlier from her bedchamber's window were filled with three other guests, one seated at each table. As she and Alice walked over to an empty table at the garden's edge, Alice pointed out each guest in turn with a running commentary; the daughter had definitely inherited her mother's garrulousness.

"That man sitting over there is Stanley Bogart. He often stays with us, although he usually takes his day meals in his room. I think the fair weather was too much to resist, even for him. He's a very good pianist. See his hands?" She rolled her eyes under cast-down lids in the man's direction. "Look how long his fingers are. We have an old baby grand piano that we keep outside the conference room—we use it for parties—and if Stanley is staying with us, he often plays it."

"That's nice of him."

"Yes. He also tells us when it needs tuning. He's very helpful that way. But he really deserves a concert grand piano to play on. I wish we had one. Maybe later we'll get one and trade in the smaller one. I have it on my wish list for one of the things we need to make us top-tier."

Jessica took a good look at the pianist. He was a serious-looking man who appeared to be in his mid or early thirties. He was slightly chubby in his build, but as Alice described, his hands were extremely long and thin; they looked as though they were well able to straddle a good length of keys of any piano keyboard.

"I guess this is a peaceful spot for him to vacation. Does he compose, or does he perform?"

"I think he does some of both." Alice whispered, "He usually stays with us when he knows that lady over there is also going to be here." She turned her head toward a young woman who was sitting in front of a neglected pot of tea and cup while she wrote feverishly in a notebook. "That's Frankie Alexis. She's a writer. Have you read any of her books?"

The woman was totally engrossed in entering notations in her notebook. At times, she clipped extra sheets to the notebook with paper clips. She did so with ferocity, so that some of the clips she grabbed from a little tray on the table flew out of her hands. And it looked as though one or two might inadvertently land in her teacup, which she continued to ignore. She looked younger than the pianist, but only slightly so. She had shoulder-length, brown hair and occasionally pushed strands of it away from her face with an annoyed gesture.

"No. Her name isn't familiar to me."

"Oh, it isn't?"

"What type of books does she write?"

"Crime dramas. I guess you'd call them thrillers to be more accurate. The violence—blood and guts and all that—is a little too much for me, but my brother, Joel, loves them. He says they're a lot better than others he's read. And he reads a lot of those types of stories, so I guess he knows what he's talking about. But as I said, not for *my* taste." She shuddered visibly, shaking her shoulders and rattling her teeth as if a cold wind had blown past her. "Anyway, I think Mr. Bogart is *sweet* on Ms. Alexis. But I don't think he has a chance, if you *know* what I mean."

They moved past the pianist and the writer and had almost made it by the last occupied table, which Alice was nonchalantly skirting, when the elderly woman sitting there looked up at them with eyes blazing with curiosity.

"Alice, is this a new guest?" the woman asked.

Jessica had no doubt that the question was rhetorical. She was sure this occupant of one of Brenda's prized harp-backed chairs had every current guest of Castle Ryan cataloged in her head. The woman was stocky. She was wearing pumps and stockings; those items of clothing worked hard to contain the bulk of her heavy limbs and feet. She wore a formal suit of tweed cloth and the fabric seemed too heavy to wear for the current temperature. On the lapel of her too tight jacket was an antique timepiece. It harkened back to a former age, before digital watches and cell phones made the exact time in any zone immediately available. The watch hung from a short gold fob. But it added a touch of elegance to the woman's otherwise well-worn suit.

"Good afternoon, Mrs. Stanwich. I hadn't wanted to disturb you."

"You wouldn't do that, dear."

"How are you doing?" Alice asked, once it was clear there was no way she and Jessica would be able to pass by without stopping to chat.

"Very well. Very well now, my dear, if I do say so myself. To be honest I was feeling a bit *peevish* a little earlier. I usually do at this time of day. That's why I so enjoy taking my tea just about now. And where else to do so? Isn't that right, dear?"

"Yes," Alice agreed.

"And who is this young lady with you, Alice?"

"This is Dr. Jessica Shepard. Dr. Shepard, Mrs. Amy Stanwich."

"Hello, Mrs. Stanwich," Jessica said. "Are you enjoying your stay here?"

"Here? Oh me, no. Good gracious, no. I'm not *staying* here. I'm just enjoying my tea and the gardens as I like to do. I have my own cottage on the edge of the property." She raised up an elephantine head, which was covered in tight, grayish-white curls, to get an even better look at the new arrival. And then she looked out and pointed with her forefinger back beyond the patio, over the greenery behind them. "My cottage is back past these grounds."

"Mrs. Stanwich likes to have her afternoon tea with us most days," Alice said, adding her own explanation to that of Amy's.

Jessica wondered how many times Alice was waylaid this way while leading guests to their tables, and she admired the younger Ryan's ability to handle a likely repetitive interruption in her daily routine with such aplomb.

"That's right, Alice. I do."

Amy turned her head back to face Jessica. "You see, the Ryans were kind enough to purchase some of my land some ways back. Now that, thanks to them, I'm a woman of independent means, as they say, I can treat myself accordingly. And I so enjoy doing so." She smiled broadly at Alice. "Well, I won't keep you dears. I'm sure you would like to get to your table and enjoy your lunch, Dr. Shepard. And I know that Alice has a lot to do helping Bevin and Brenda run this big place. It must take so much effort to do so."

Amy looked back at her teacup to signal that she had

concluded the interview and added generous helpings of milk and sugar to the dark-black liquid. Then almost as an afterthought, she murmured mainly to herself, "My mother always taught me to add the milk first to prevent any cracking of fine bone china cups. Remember that, dear. One should always take good care of one's fine possessions."

Amy took a sip from the cup. Then she lifted the lid of the white, porcelain teapot, looking deep inside as though to see how many cups were still available to relax her peevishness.

Alice settled Jessica at her table, handed her one of the bills of fare that were neatly stacked between the salt and pepper shakers, and retreated to her post inside the dining room, having introduced the inn's three colorful guests to the latest arrival.

Jessica looked over the menu. The option of tea, which Amy was so obviously enjoying, had a place of prominence at the very top of the list of selections. Described as a large pot of Irish tea with a choice of various specificities and flavors, it could be accompanied by a platter of small sandwiches. *That's just what I want,* Jessica thought. Hunger was starting to rear its ugly head for her. She placed her lunch order with Lora, the young girl serving the tables who Alice had sent over to Jessica. Lora looked eager to take whatever directions she could get from Alice. She had been previously splitting her time between the other two guests while Jessica, Alice, and Amy had been talking.

As Jessica waited for her sandwiches to arrive, she drank the tea that Lora provided. The drink was hot and bracing, but she didn't have the courage to add milk to it as was the local custom and satisfied herself with a mere single teaspoon of sugar.

Because she had almost a full day left to explore the grounds before Aspen and Thornes arrived, Jessica decided that after lunch she would stroll around them. She wanted to get a better look at the native flora than she had from the window of Sean Telford's car on their drive up to the castle. She especially wanted to look at the abundant yellow gorse she had glimpsed from the car.

On the table, behind the menus, was a printed brochure of the castle and its property. It included a simply diagrammed map of walking trails that meandered through the grounds. She would start with one of those. Looking over the map, she saw that the property stretched far back behind the patio, past the boxwood-rose parterres, through a grassy clearing, and then onto more wooded sections of land. The map noted the paths to be well marked and easy to follow for any guest unfamiliar with them as she was. The brochure also noted that the grounds were under the management of the head gardener, Mr. Alvin Hill, who had been in charge of them for many years.

The pamphlet, though printed, had a homemade feel to it. On the front page was a picture of the four Ryans: Bevin, Brenda, Joel, and Alice. They were standing proudly in a straight line in front of the huge entrance door to Castle Ryan. The picture must have been taken a little while ago because Brenda and Alice appeared somewhat younger than they had seemed to Jessica on a first meeting.

The picture was an opportunity to see what father and son looked like. Bevin Ryan was a tall man who towered over Brenda and Alice, and even over his son, Joel, who was still taller than his mother and sister. Bevin was an attractive man. His rugged features seemed to retain a type of vigor despite his older age, evinced by the gray hair at his temples. Joel had dark hair; the red color of the maternal side of the family had obviously missed the son. The four had been positioned stiffly in front of the castle for the promotional photo, but they stood next to each other in front of the redbrick building as though welcoming guests into their own home.

Jessica turned back to the diagramed walking paths and decided not to delay a minute longer her exploratory walk about the place. She tossed back what was left of her tea sandwiches, signed the bill for her lunch, took one last drop of tea, and stood up from the table. As she did, she saw Stanley, the pianist, and Amy, the elderly local, spy one last glance at her.

But Frankie, the crime-story writer, was too absorbed in her frenetic writing to notice Jessica. Frankie was scribbling rapidly in her notebook and only stopped at that moment to impatiently hurl away from her a pen that must have run out of ink. And then she pulled out a new one from her purse with almost no break in her writing as Jessica walked away from the patio and toward the well-tended rose garden behind Castle Ryan.

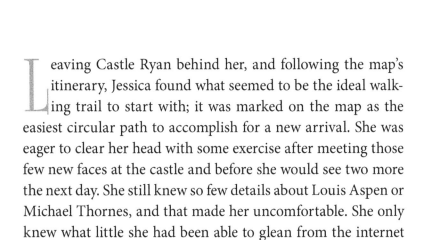

Four
A Walk in the Woods

eaving Castle Ryan behind her, and following the map's itinerary, Jessica found what seemed to be the ideal walking trail to start with; it was marked on the map as the easiest circular path to accomplish for a new arrival. She was eager to clear her head with some exercise after meeting those few new faces at the castle and before she would see two more the next day. She still knew so few details about Louis Aspen or Michael Thornes, and that made her uncomfortable. She only knew what little she had been able to glean from the internet before she left home for Ireland.

Tom Martine hadn't heard of any significant concerns about either of them. But he had admitted that he might have been somewhat cavalier in mentioning Jessica and Alain's colorful history to Aspen. It had been clear that her friend, the investigative journalist, had been most interested in extolling his two friends' skills, and perhaps also in unloading the producer onto them rather than being burdened with Louis Aspen himself.

There was as yet no strong reason for her own concern because it was just to be a meet-and-greet between them; it in no way obligated her to any agreement. But it was still her responsibility to consider the implications of the potential project carefully. And a quiet walk in the woods, unencumbered by the need to talk to anyone else, was Jessica's tried-and-true method of examining possibilities to reach the best decision without being swayed by anyone else's opinion.

Her last time to think alone had been so short. She had just returned from Paris—a trip that had started with the expectation of reconnecting with Alain, only to once again be enveloped by what they felt was their mutual duty to solve a murder case that on the surface had seemed undecipherable. The fact that the deceased had been a close acquaintance of Alain's daughter, Odette, had brought very close to home the need to solve the case.

She sighed but then remembered that the trip had ended with such a sweet time for herself and Alain to finally establish some degree of normalcy and clarity in their relationship. They reached acceptance that their bond, although loving, would be stretched like a rubber band by distance—his place was in Montreal and hers in Connecticut. They agreed the best way to go on was to accept there would be hiatuses and reestablishments of their closeness. They were both set in their ways and old enough to treasure what they had. And they were determined to make it work in any form that it took.

Now here were the new, complicating factors: a producer and a screenwriter intent on having hers and Alain's investigative exploits publicized in a television project for all to visualize, no doubt in all its gory details. She had no idea if Alain would accept that concept at its core. But she didn't want to reject the project outright—at least not yet. Aspen's encouragement had been so vigorously energetic. She was fully prepared to listen to the man in person and to his many ideas; if they were interesting enough, only then would she approach Alain and try to get his buy-in. She rationalized that if she had immediately turned Aspen down, he would most likely have only gone on to Alain and approached him instead. And something inside her wanted to be the first to hear Aspen out.

Jessica broke out of her deep study as the harsh sound of a dead branch from a tree in front of her suddenly snapped off its trunk with a gust of wind. It dropped on the path just in front of her, missing her only by a few feet. She jumped back and then looked around her and suddenly realized that she had allowed her thoughts to wander so much that she was now off her original path. There were no identifying trail markers immediately in front of her, and the last one she remembered passing was far behind her. She had no alternative but to continue walking on.

She needed to try to find an identifiable landmark or some signage to lead her in the right direction. She knew that if she kept her wits about her, she would have no difficulty relating the path to the map she still clutched in her hand. She walked on until she finally found a sign, which identified the current path on her map as somewhat longer than the original one she had been on. She studied the map and looked at her watch, computing that she could still complete it and return to the castle before dark. "I might as well go on instead of trying to retrace my steps back to the patio. I bet Amy Stanwich's eager and interested eyes are still waiting for me to come back," she muttered to herself. "Maybe I should be grateful for that." She chuckled and shook her head. *"Chicken! Bok bok!"*

The new path was somewhat challenging and led her down a meandrous road that curved through the trees. She passed overgrown shrubs and sturdy trees with thick leaves that formed a dark canopy over her head as they met each other from either side of the road. However, the canopy provided some welcome relief from the afternoon sun, which broke through the few clouds in the sky. After a while she almost started to enjoy herself. The white of the clouds, the blue of the sky, and the green of the leaves formed a colorful potpourri, making Jessica get lost in nature's beauty and forget, for the time being, her worry about not making it back to the castle before dark. She felt the beauty of the tableau was payment for having to traverse a distance longer than expected. She continued following her new path as it went on and on.

Then, up ahead, she saw a swath of white that couldn't belong to any cloud formation; it was just too low in the sky. Moving closer, she realized she was spying a small Victorian home. It was two stories in height with a flat-roof sun terrace that was sure to allow an excellent view of any approaching intruders, invited or not.

The front of the house had a gravel entrance, much smaller than that of Castle Ryan. There was a black, metal name plaque to the right of the door. Jessica looked ahead, back, and to each side of her; no one was watching. She decided to indulge her curiosity and take a closer look at the lettering on the plaque. Walking over to it, acutely aware of the crunch of the coarse gravel under her shoes, she saw the name: Stanwich Cottage.

"This must be the one 'on the edge of the property' that Amy mentioned," Jessica said to herself. "There couldn't be another with the same name within the limits of the estate. It would be too coincidental for it to be other than Amy's home." Jessica scanned the map for any description of the house but couldn't find any; but then, thinking about it, that would be a surprise. "Amy mentioned that she sold some of her land to the Ryans, but she described the cottage as her own."

Taking another furtive look to her right and left and confirming that no one else was around, she made the quick decision to grab a peek into the ground-floor windows of Stanwich

Cottage. There was a large, mullioned window to the right of the door, where the shade wasn't pulled down as far as all the others. She moved over to it and peered in beneath the bottom edge of the shade. It caused her to twist her body over like an agile contortionist. She silently prayed that she wouldn't keel over and end up splayed headlong among the shrubbery that ran along the edges of the trim cottage.

Through the glass, Jessica could make out a few pieces of dark-wood and upholstered furniture, and an upright piano stood against the far wall. Its keyboard cover was folded down over the keys, and there was no open music on the music shelf as though no one was in the habit of playing the instrument regularly. Nothing appeared out of order. She was unable to see much more of interest, and certainly nothing other than what she might expect in the home of the elderly woman who likely resided there.

"Ruff. Ruff. Ruff." It was the unmistakable barking of a dog. The high-pitched sound told her heightened senses it must belong to a tiny breed. Controlling her movements with almost scientific precision while she continued looking inside, she saw the pane of glass was soon the only thing separating her from a small black terrier, which was now frantically jumping up and down on a chair. It had a definitely unfriendly look in its eyes, and its snarling jaw was an extremely unpleasant sight to behold. It appeared as though any minute the small dog would jump from the shelter of the chair, run across the room, and confront her directly on the other side of the window.

"Nice doggie, nice doggie, nice doggie," she mouthed, backing slowly away from the window. She controlled her fear of the animal with the slow breathing techniques she had trained herself to use in such situations.

She continued to move farther back from the cottage. "Well, I think you've indulged your investigative proclivity enough for your own good—at least for now. That has certainly been decided for you," she muttered, shaking her head up and down while she kept her eyes focused on the cottage she was retreating from. "Better to take curiosity down another avenue for the present. After all, it's only my first day here." She moved still farther away from the front of the house. Finally, the hysterical barking dissipated as she turned around and crunched back over the gravel drive, now in full and steady retreat. She quickly found her way back to the walking path to continue on her exploration about the grounds, hopefully not to run into any other animals bigger than a chipmunk.

As she plodded along, Jessica mulled over in her mind the connection between the two existing residences on the Ryans and the neighboring properties. Sean and Millie, her first new acquaintances on arrival in Dalkey, had alluded to some of the more colorful aspects of the estate's history. She remembered them telling her the castle had once been owned by a very rich gentleman who had been unhappy about his wife's literary aspirations, and then he had lost her under suspicious circumstances.

Jessica wondered if Stanwich Cottage might have been part of the original estate. And if so, perhaps, it had served as a type of sanctuary for fulfillment of the literary passions of the former lady of the manor: the passions that had been no longer indulged by the woman's husband. Maybe she had even gone there to write in private by herself, away from her husband's watchful eye. Or perhaps she had done more there that was scandalous for the times.

Certainly, the cottage looked old enough to have been built contemporaneously to the major building on the estate. If so, how the cottage might have passed to Amy and so much of the land around it to the Ryans Jessica couldn't know. Perhaps financial reversals had encouraged the elderly woman to sell off her parcel of land to the Ryans. At least on a first meeting, Amy seemed quite content with the current arrangement, enjoying her daily tea on the inn's patio. Perhaps it might not have been a financial decision. Maybe it was just a cordial agreement between the two parties, relieving an older woman's burden of responsibility as a landowner to a family only too eager to enlarge the property around their inn for the enjoyment of potential guests like Jessica. It was a question that would have to remain on the backburner for now.

Jessica let her feverish speculations fly away from her with the breeze that was just starting to blow up for the night. She determined to concentrate less on the question of land owner-ship and more on that of expeditiously finding her way back to the safety of the inn. It was getting closer to dinnertime and she was getting back the hearty appetite that the tea sandwiches had only temporarily assuaged. Besides, she was eager to see what would be provided in the dining room that was so elegantly outfitted earlier in the day. After all, her food and lodging were being generously provided by the team of Aspen and Thornes. She might as well make the best of the situation before meeting them tomorrow and possibly blowing them off for good.

Five
Dinner at Seven

At seven o'clock in the evening, Jessica was safely back from her perambulation around the grounds of Castle Ryan. She was attired in what she thought was appropriate for dinner in the castle. She was wearing a simple black, sheath dress and a silver chain around her neck. Matching silver earrings dangled from her ears.

She entered the dining room and was greeted by a young man. His resemblance to the picture she had seen in the castle's brochure left no doubt that he was Joel Ryan, the son of the proprietors. He had an engaging smile. As she walked over to him, he said, "Dr. Shepard, I presume." The youthful grin he displayed after the delivered quip overcame the irritation that she usually felt when being subjected to one that had been applied too often for its own good. After all, he wasn't emerging from the jungle to find her; she was merely arriving for dinner. Although, when she came to think of it, at a few points on the trail about the castle's estate she did wonder if she would ever get out of the forest.

"Right on the money," she shot back, opting to follow his lead.

"Sorry. I learned that reference in school and I like to use it. Anyway, I hope it is all right with you, but since your other party won't be arriving until tomorrow, my mother thought it a good idea to seat you at a table with some other guests."

"That's fine."

"If you'd prefer to be alone, I can work it out. But I think my sister, Alice, pointed them out to you earlier—Stanley Bogart and Frankie Alexis. So it's not like you have absolutely no idea who they are. Also, just between us, I think Frankie would appreciate the extra guest at her table. So you see, I'm killing two birds with one stone. Also, most of the others tonight seem to be families, so I think my ma's suggestion will work—if it's OK with you, that is."

"Yes. That's perfectly fine with me. I'd also rather not sit alone in such a large space."

Jessica looked around the capacious dining room. It seemed even larger than it had during the day when it was still empty of any guests. Most of the tables were filled with the families Joel mentioned, though some were unoccupied. The white linen cloths covering the tables that she had noticed that afternoon now had on them small crystal vases filled with roses. Their red and pink colors exactly matched those in the bushes Jessica had seen surrounding the patio; the bushes had obviously provided the evening's copious supply. Tall candles flickered light on the polished silverware and the linen napkins of deep emerald green.

But strangely, the light from the candles seemed to play tricks on her eyes; she made the unexpected mental connection that the color of the red buds in their vases bore an eerie resemblance to the color of blood; their deep red overwhelmed the paler pink blossoms beside them. It was unnerving.

Shaking her head to remove the image, Jessica followed Joel through the room to the table where Stanley Bogart and Frankie Alexis already sat. At least for the evening meal, Frankie no longer had her pens and notebooks scattered around her. But the absence of those writing tools wasn't preventing her from studiously avoiding deep conversation with her dinner partner. She was looking about the room and had no eyes for the ardent suitor beside her.

"Ms. Alexis, Mr. Bogart, here's someone to share your table," Joel said. "This is Dr. Shepard. I'll leave you to get to know each other." He turned away on his heel and headed back to the front of the room where other guests were now arriving.

Jessica sat down between Stanley and Frankie and faced an empty space across from her. It was clear that her purpose for the evening was to serve as a physical barrier between the writer on one side of her and the pianist on the other.

"So you're a doctor," Frankie said, beginning the conversation. "Brenda Ryan's already provided me with some of the rundown about you. That woman can't resist talking, particularly to guests like me who have stayed here before. Be sure and keep whatever secrets you have away from her."

"Oh, I don't really have secrets," Jessica said, unsure exactly how best to respond.

"Well, I think we all have them. But that's OK. It was just a friendly word of advice. That's all."

"Then I appreciate that. Yes, I'm a doctor. I'm an immunologist by training. Tonight though, I'm still here as a vacationer, but I'm meeting two other guests tomorrow to discuss some business.

"Yes. Brenda's also let on that your *business* is with a television producer and a screenwriter," Frankie said. "Our proprietress is very excited about that. I think she sees the opportunity for a few good things for Castle Ryan coming out of your meeting."

"Oh, she has mentioned it?"

"Don't expect anything to remain a secret around here. As you've probably already noticed, and as I just alluded to, Brenda Ryan has difficulty controlling her tongue."

"I've been told you're a crime fiction writer, Ms. Alexis," Jessica said, trying to politely change the subject. She turned toward Stanley and said, "And you, Mr. Bogart, are a pianist."

"Oh, why don't we dispense with all the formality?" Frankie snorted and took a gulp from her water glass. "I'm Frankie, this is Stanley, and you're Jessica. If there's one thing I've learned as a writer, it's that brevity is key. OK with you?"

"That's a wonderful idea," Jessica said.

"Great," Frankie said. "So yes, I write crime fiction. I love to read them and to write them. And given a choice, I'd say that I love writing my own work rather than reading anyone else's. But that's just my opinion until I can publish more than I've done so far. But I'm always on the lookout for new character types for my books. That's why I like coming to places like this. They're great spots to scout out the local *characters*. Stanley here doesn't seem to take advantage of those types of influencers in his musical work, although I've told him he should."

"I saw at lunch that you met the local character," Stanley said, finally joining in on the conversation. "She'd be a good type for one of your books, Frankie."

"Amy Stanwich?" Jessica proffered.

"Yes. Amy Stanwich," Frankie said. "Dalkey's own Amy Stanwich. I spied her waylay you on your way to lunch. I knew you wouldn't get away. Alice doesn't know how to handle her. Amy dares not interrupt *me* while I'm writing. I get some of my best ideas while I'm eating and drinking. I don't know why, but I do. And once I'm absorbed in my plots, I can't have anyone drag me out of them. It damages the writing if I come out of my zone. I lose my place. Anyway, I've got to find *a place* for her in one of my next books. That's *one* thing you're right about, Stanley."

"I think I came across her home when I was out walking the trails behind the castle," Jessica said. "A small, white cottage."

"Stanwich Cottage? Two stories with a flat roof in the back of the estate?"

"That's it."

Stanley broke in, obviously eager not to be left out of the deepening conversation between the two women at the table. "Amy sold some of her land to the Ryans. That's why she likes to have her tea every day at the castle, usually on the patio if the weather allows so she can survey the gardens."

"That's right, Stanley," Frankie said. "You see more than I give you credit for."

"Well, I don't often take lunch out of my room. But when I do, and I'm eating on the patio, she's always there. Usually I just take a sandwich on a tray up to my room or down by the castle's piano outside the conference room. I like to keep busy even when I'm staying here on vacation. And I find it more efficient that way—to eat while I work. I'm studying biographies of some of the great composers such as Robert Schumann. Studying great musical minds gives me my inspiration. And their history makes for some interesting discussions with the students I teach from time to time."

"Let's hope you don't end up like Schumann, Stanley," Frankie said. "Even though you can be annoying, I'd hate for you to end up that way."

"Oh, I won't. Don't worry about that." He looked down at his hands for a few moments as though contemplating something very concerning, perhaps the final days of deteriorating health and eventual death of Robert Schumann, the early nineteen-century German composer who died at forty-six years. Then he looked back up and said, "Jessica, I've known

Frankie for some time, so I'm used to her sarcasm. Don't let her unnerve you."

"I won't." It struck Jessica that there was so little comparison with the ribbing she had witnessed between Millie and Sean to this sharper back-and-forth between Frankie and Stanley. In this case, it was clearly Frankie who seemed to have the rougher edge.

The writer must have sensed Jessica's discomfort.

"Let's change the subject," Frankie said abruptly, saving Jessica from having to struggle to latch onto a less depressing topic for conversation. "I also spied you admiring the gardens. You like flowers, I imagine. I'm not big on them myself. I prefer birds, if I'm going to spend time goggling at nature. But I know some people enjoy looking at flowers. Though I don't have much use for them in my books. Birds are more interesting to me for that purpose. They can almost be characters themselves."

"Yes. I do love flowers. Although I do like birds too. I have a large garden at home, so I know how difficult it is to keep it looking so beautiful. The many plantings around the estate are quite impressive. And they're so varied. I saw a good many of them when I walked around the grounds. I read the castle keeps a gardener on staff full time."

Stanley said, "Alvin Hill. He's been around here for as long as I can remember. Frankie, that's another character you can put in one of your books."

"Why? I like him. He does his job well. I wouldn't want to kill him off or make him one of my murderers."

"Well, just don't try to give him any *ideas* about his gardens, or he'll bite your head off like he nearly did me. That's all I'm saying."

"Now Stanley, what does a *pianist* know about gardening?"

"I didn't say I was *an expert*."

"Well, I'm glad of that. Don't be ridiculous. I'm amazed he didn't run you over with his wheelbarrow for your presumption!" Frankie's irritation with her table partner had crept into her voice. She took the emerald green linen napkin, which had been carefully constructed like a piece of origami into a conical arrangement on her plate, and practically snapped it straight out onto her lap.

Jessica was just glad Frankie hadn't snapped the napkin into Stanley's face. The pianist looked positively crestfallen at the writer's last retort.

"I was just trying to be helpful, Frankie."

"Just leave Alvin alone. That's all I'm telling you. He knows what he's about. He doesn't need to take his directions from you."

"OK. OK. I'm sorry. I didn't mean to ruffle your feathers."

Further discussion was interrupted by the serendipitous appearance of Lora, who had served them at lunch and was back on duty for the evening meal. Castle Ryan had an excellent cook. The food seemed to smooth over the controversial aspects of the predinner conversation.

They started with a selection of smoked salmon the color of marmalade, sliced paper thin, with pungent green capers and wedges of bright-red tomatoes garnishing the edges of the white china plates. White wine filled the crystal goblets that had sat empty next to the water glasses and now were replete with the pale-yellow, fragrant alcohol. Black cod followed the first course and was sautéed to perfection in creamy butter. The accompanying vegetables were so fresh that Jessica wondered if they came from a large kitchen garden on the estate, most likely also tended to by the enterprising gardener, Alvin Hill.

The meal finally ended with a delicate flan, its crispy, brown crust flaking delicately when the spoon cracked it open to reveal the sweet, oozing concoction beneath the surface. The luscious dessert was accompanied by strong, aromatic coffee served in a tall, silver coffee urn that reflected the fading light of the dwindling candles on the table.

Having so pleasantly satisfied her hunger and made the closer acquaintance of the writer and the pianist, despite the duo's confrontational interchange, Jessica left the dining room at the completion of the meal. She climbed the elegant wooden staircase back to her room to get a good night's sleep before she would have to wrangle with the producer and the screenwriter the next day.

Six

A Disturbance
in the Night

Sleep did not come easily for Jessica. She tossed and turned under the heavy coverlet; at times it seemed as if the bedclothes were a shroud encasing her body within their depths. Her mind was in turmoil. Whether from the evening's rich dishes, the two glasses of wine she drank, or just from sleeping in a foreign bed, she couldn't stop thinking about what she would say to Aspen and Thornes the next day. She came no closer in her mind to how much of her privacy she wanted to give up, especially to a television audience, should the project ever come to fruition. She wouldn't allow herself to consider what Alain's opinion would be, although if she were honest with herself, she could guess he would be unlikely to view it positively.

"Well, no sense in worrying about it any longer," she said out loud, impatient with her insomnia. Exhaustion and frustration were becoming so overwhelming that she finally forced herself into total immobility. And at last, the lack of body motion perversely allowed her to relax. The four-poster bed and its sateen, quilted coverlet were suddenly comforting. She pulled the quilt up to her chin and then over the bridge of her nose. She settled back into the nurturing softness of the thick mattress and feather pillows and finally fell asleep.

Creak. Creak. The noises roused her from sleep. She opened her eyes and struggled to clear them as well as her foggy head. She thought she had just closed her eyes. She could only have been asleep a few minutes. But the luminous digital clock on the bedside table read two o'clock. So she must have been asleep for a good few hours. *Creak. Creak.* She heard it again. This time she was sure of it. It sounded like the noise made by someone treading softly on old floorboards. Her confused brain worked diligently to create a mental image of the long corridor outside her room. She tried to remember if she had seen any other doors in the hall to other rooms near hers.

But try as she would, all she could remember was that silly, carved owl perched on its tall plinth, the one she had first spotted when turning around the corner when Brenda led her to this room in the right wing of the castle. It had taken up all her attention at the time. Now she couldn't recall what else had been in the corridor.

She had definitely locked the door to her room after coming back from dinner. She was certain of that. But as she lay in bed, that assurance seemed to fly away as easily as her remembrance of what else she had noticed in the corridor outside.

"Doesn't hurt to double-check," she whispered to herself. "Maybe it's another guest coming back late." But none of the other diners seemed the type to be traipsing around the hotel at two o'clock in the morning. It must be one of the staff. *That's it.* But why would they be in one of the guest wings at this time of night? Putting out newspapers for the next day? The thoughts floated through her head, accentuated by the knowledge that she was alone in her room in an old castle. Then she suddenly remembered the colorful story Sean and Millie had told her.

"Oh, Jessica, you're such a wimp." This time she said it out loud without any hint of a whisper. She threw back the covers in total irritation with her own pusillanimous behavior and got out of the four-poster bed. She was now fully awake. She switched on the bedside lamp. Although feeble, the illumination managed to meagerly flood the room and was enough to confirm the bedroom door was solidly closed. The room appeared exactly as it had looked before she had fallen off to sleep. She shoved her feet into her bedroom slippers that were beside the bed, stubbing her toes painfully in the process, and she went over to the door.

"Aah! Aah!" The screams came from behind the door and out of a woman's throat. There could be no mistaking that fact.

Without a moment's hesitation, all trepidation now gone from her, Jessica unbolted the door with one jerking motion of the heavy lock and the door threw open. The hall was dark, but she could make out that it was Frankie standing directly in front of her. Frankie was also dressed in a nightgown, and several feet behind her was Stanley, also in pajamas. His mouth was gaping widely, and incongruously it struck Jessica that he bore a comical resemblance to a bird—and not any wise owl. That answered the question of whether or not she was the only guest on the corridor; her dinner companions had obviously both been placed in the same wing of the castle. But they were now no longer safely ensconced in their individual rooms for the night; they were all haunting the right wing of Castle Ryan.

"Frankie? Frankie? Was that you?" Stanley shouted. The pitch of his voice jumped from baritone to tenor, and almost to falsetto, from the first to the second repetition of Frankie's name. "You made such an awful sound. It was frightening!"

Frankie gazed behind her at him, as though she couldn't

digest what he was saying. Then she looked at Jessica, finally noticing her presence, and asked, "Did I really make that horrible noise? I can't believe it."

"Frankie, did you see something that frightened you?" Jessica asked. "I also heard you scream."

"I must have." She shook her head as if to clear her thinking from an overwhelming fog. "But now I can't believe I did. I heard definite creaking. I do remember that. *That* was the very first thing I heard when I woke up. I went out to see what it was."

"So did I," Jessica blurted out. "It also woke me."

"Me too," Stanley added.

"Well, at least we're all on the same page," Frankie said, confidence slowly returning to the deep timbre of her voice. "I looked out of my room and then I saw *her*."

"Who?" Jessica and Stanley asked almost simultaneously.

"*Evelyn!*"

"Who's Evelyn?" Jessica asked.

"Evelyn's a *ghost*."

"Oh, come on, Frankie! Really! You're being so *dramatic*!" Stanley said with surprising vigor. "That's so unlike you! And you call yourself a writer of crime fiction! Maybe you should try your hand in the *theater*." He drawled out the last word in a sarcastic manner that shocked Jessica. She wouldn't have expected it of him.

"Now don't you use that tone of voice with me! I am not one of your music students you can push around, although it's more likely they push you around! Ask any local around here if you don't believe me. If you would just accept that there's a world around you that is a little bit more *mysterious* than your limited, eighty-eight piano keys, you'd understand what I'm saying. I'm telling you I saw her. Just like you'd expect that she would look. *Pale. Very pale.* Dressed in a muslin dress, which was the color of old paper, turned almost creamy with age. And her dark hair, all swirled up high on the top of her head. Although no, not exactly like that." She furrowed her brow and shook her head. "Not exactly. She was hazier, almost ethereal, like a vapor that melted into the thin air." She waved her hand in a circle in front of her face, waited a moment, and then said, "But I'm positive I saw her. I wasn't dreaming. I couldn't have been. No."

Jessica looked at the owl, still fixed on its plinth in the darkened corridor. She was unable to believe that the local legend that Sean and Millie had apprised her of could be one and the same background for whatever Frankie thought she witnessed. She put her hand on Frankie's bare arm. She could feel the gooseflesh on the other woman's cool extremity.

"Frankie, do you think you might have thought the owl in the dark was an *apparition?*" Jessica nodded her head toward the carved bird, silhouetted in the dark. "Or maybe someone was playing a joke on you? Could it have been that? Brenda told me her children used to dress the owl up when they were younger. Maybe you saw some of the costumes that someone might have gotten a hold of and now removed?" Jessica peered to her right and her left. "Although the corridor clearly looks empty now. I'll grant you that."

"No. I haven't left this spot since I saw her. There was no one else in the hall. I'm sure of that." Frankie stomped her right foot impatiently so that the floorboards of the corridor now tapped out rather than creaked a sharp, staccato rhythm. "Oh, I don't know. Maybe I'm *losing* it." She bit her lower lip. "I have been writing a lot, and I have gotten a bit lost in my characters and my plot. I've done that before. I may be more tired than I think I am. And I did have a cocktail before dinner and then the wine that was served with dinner." She shook her head again. "I don't know. Maybe you're right."

Jessica let go of Frankie's arm. "Well, it's all quiet now. What do you say we all go back to bed? That's the only reasonable thing we can do at the moment. We can try to figure it out in the morning when none of us is so tired as we are now."

"Good idea," Frankie said with a deep sigh. She turned away from Jessica and Stanley to head back to her room.

"Frankie, do you want me to check your room before you go in there?" Stanley asked tentatively.

"No."

"I'm happy to do it if it would make you feel better and make it easier for you to fall back to sleep. I don't want you to be afraid."

"Afraid? No. No. Don't be silly. I'm fine. The doctor's right. Let's all get some sleep." She stalked off to her room, closing the door firmly behind her. A moment later, they heard the bolt slide back into place.

"Well, I guess that's my cue," Stanley said as he sighed and went back to his room. "She's never willing to take my help when she knows about it."

Jessica, left alone in the corridor, hesitated for a full minute. Then she decided she should take her own good advice, which she had just successfully given the other two audience members of the early morning's eerie entertainment. She went back to her bedchamber and closed the door behind her. Then she bolted the lock as forcefully as she had heard Frankie do before. She went back to the large four-poster and got into bed, once again pulling the coverlet over her. But she knew the sleep that would come to her would be of a very different kind to what she had experienced just before the strange events in the corridor.

Seven
Jessica Meets
the Duumvirate

essica woke up as the first rays of sun pierced the gap between the window curtains of her bedchamber. At first, she was unsure if the strange events of the early morning hours had truly happened or they had merely been a dream provoked by unfamiliar surroundings. As she lay in bed, she went over them in her mind as if they were file folders she needed to catalog before she could even begin to understand their significance. She mentally arranged them, one by one in sequence, until each had its perfect position in her brain. First there had been creaking of the floorboards outside her room, then the appearance of Frankie and Stanley, and finally the confession by Frankie of witnessing the apparition of a woman, probable or not.

After doing her mental organization, she was convinced her memory was accurate and the events had happened. But if asked to guess which of her dining partners from the last night's convivial meal would have been disturbed by a ghostly apparition, she would have picked Stanley and not Frankie. He seemed more impressionable. But Frankie knew the story being circulated, in obviously widening circles, about the woman she called *Evelyn,* who Jessica surmised was the name of the castle's mistress who died those many years ago under unclear circumstances. Frankie was a writer, and from what Jessica had learned so far, Evelyn had been an aspiring one as well. Could it be that Evelyn had reached out across time and space to find a sympathetic soul? Or was that all just too preposterous to contemplate for anyone of a logical and analytic mind as Jessica liked to consider herself.

"Really, Jessica? What are you thinking?" she muttered. She continued shooting questions at herself so that the sound of her words would allow her brain to better dissect what it was she was considering. "How can I let myself get so caught up in local legend? What's wrong with me? The Castle Ryan's old, creaking floorboards and paneled corridors are making me credit things that I would quickly toss out if I was at a modern hotel. Aspen and Thornes are playing their cards correctly by suggesting this location for discussion of fictional television. The castle's aura is getting to me and making me outright fanciful!"

It is so unlike me, she thought. *Better get out of bed and come back to reality.*

She threw back the covers and jumped out of bed. Puzzlement over the incidents in the corridor was quickly replaced by anxiety over her upcoming meeting with Aspen and Thornes. They were sure to arrive today if they hadn't already arrived late last night. She hoped they had. They couldn't expect her to continue to while away the days at Castle Ryan waiting for them to make an appearance. She also couldn't imagine they would want to foot the bill for it.

Jessica headed to the bathroom to shower. The feeling of hot water gently massaging her tight muscles would relax her and help to focus her mind on the anticipated meeting. She was eager to turn on the tap and indulge in some good old hydrotherapy. The room was renovated and had all the modern conveniences but retained classical features not at odds with what she had seen so far. Shiny, sea-green tiles ran up the walls above dark-wood wainscoting. There was a bulky, chrome, heated-towel rack in one corner of the room, and the hot and cold handles of the sink and bath were white porcelain with black lettering in bold relief. Gratified to find that the hot handles produced hot water and the cold ones gave out cold water, Jessica took her shower, dried herself with a heated towel, and pulled on the thick, white-cotton robe that hung from a hook behind the wooden door.

She went over to the large armoire that she had used to hang her clothes the day before. She opened the elegant piece of furniture and reviewed the selection she had brought with her. She found a black pantsuit and white, satin, sleeveless blouse. As she studied the suit for any possible creases, she remembered Amy Stanwich's attire. She was pretty sure that was one woman who would never wear *pants* even if she called then *slacks*. Jessica had no elegant, classic timepiece to attach to her own suit lapel. She pulled the white blouse on and then the black suit, and she found black pumps for a touch of formality. She would save the cotton socks and sneakers for the next long walk around the estate. She grabbed her purse and left the room. She was determined to hunt down Brenda Ryan to learn if the producing and screenwriting team had finally arrived at Castle Ryan.

Jessica descended the central staircase, after avoiding with determination the carved wooden owl in the corridor. She willed herself not to check any dark corners for potential otherworldly appearances of any kind. But when she reached the ground floor, she saw that Brenda was not on duty in the main entrance hall; instead, Jessica got her first introduction to the woman's husband, Bevin Ryan. He looked just as depicted in Castle Ryan's brochure, except the man behind the reception desk was much grayer than he had appeared in reproduced form. He was as tall as the printed picture had shown and he towered over the desk, which his wife had manned with her more diminutive form the day before.

"Good morning," he said when Jessica approached.

"Good morning. I'm Jessica Shepard. You must be Bevin Ryan."

"That I am."

"It's very nice to meet you. I've already had the pleasure of meeting your wife, daughter, and son."

"The whole family then? I see. Well, isn't that kind of you to put it that way? Yes. This is a family operation. It's the best way to run an old place like this. That's what I think. That it is. And what may I do for you now?"

"I'm expecting two guests who are joining me: Louis Aspen and Michael Thornes. They should be here by now. At least, I hope so." Jessica held her breath. She didn't know what she would do if those two men still hadn't shown up. But she needn't have worried.

"Yes. I'm familiar with who they are. Mr. Aspen and Mr. Thornes arrived late last night. Shall I send them to you when I see them this morning? I would imagine that they'll be down from their rooms shortly."

Jessica breathed a deep sigh of relief. "Yes. That's great. I would appreciate that."

"Now where would you be planning to spend your morning so I can find you once they come down? It's easy to get lost in a big place like this. There's a lot of nooks and crannies to it."

"Oh, it's such a nice day. I think I'll have some coffee and wait for them on the patio outside, behind the castle. Would that be convenient for you to have them join me there?"

"That's a fine idea on such a beautiful day. I'll have them look for you there when they come down."

"By the way, Mr. Ryan—?"

"Yes?"

"I was wondering. Did you happen to hear any particular *disturbance* very early this morning?"

"Disturbance? No?" His brow wrinkled, creating two comma-shaped lines between his shaggy eyebrows. "Were any of the guests making too much noise for you? You must let me know if anyone inconveniences you or interrupts your sleep. I'll put a stop to that directly. That's what I'm here for. You mustn't be afraid to get me involved in anything like that."

"No. No. I didn't mean to imply something like that. I just wondered if you had heard any noises. It's an old house after all. I guess that's all it was that disturbed me."

"Yes. It is old. That's true. It gives us a good creak or two now and then. But you'll get used to that. We have to, don't we? We don't have any other choice sometimes. So don't you worry about that. Actually, most of our guests say they like the grand old atmosphere; that's why they stay with us. At least, that's what they tell me. We consider this house as a symbol of fortitude. Yes. That's right. That's how I like to think about it. It's got a history to it."

"Yes. I agree with you on that point. Well, you will find me when Mr. Aspen and Mr. Thornes come down, won't you?"

"Of course, I will. Don't worry about that either."

Jessica left him and made her way toward the patio. From what Bevin Ryan had said—or hadn't said—he wasn't aware of Frankie's frightening experience in the early morning hours. Obviously, Frankie hadn't mentioned it to him if she had already come down from her room. Maybe Frankie didn't want to look foolish either, discussing what she had or hadn't seen. From what Jessica had learned from her brief acquaintance with the crime writer, the woman took great pride in her independence. Maybe Frankie thought the proprietors would think she was just living out one of her own plots—life imitating fiction?

Unless Frankie was still up in her room, intending to broach the subject with the proprietors later that day. But wasn't it really Frankie's decision to make and not Jessica's? After all, it had been Frankie and not Jessica who had witnessed whatever Frankie thought she had seen. In any case, the event, whatever it was, was now over. As Jessica hadn't seen anything out of the ordinary herself, she had best let it go.

Jessica entered the dining room and was greeted by Lora. Neither Alice nor Joel Ryan was anywhere in sight this morning.

"Good morning. Here for breakfast?" Lora asked.

The girl seemed less flustered this morning than she had the day before. Jessica assumed most of the guests slept in later than was Jessica's custom and that Lora likely preferred the less hectic pace of the early morning hours around the castle. Even the girl's appearance was more put together than it had been the day before. Lora's hair was neatly arranged in a braid wound over her head. Her serving dress was crisp and clean, unsullied by any splashes from any of the servings she would be dishing out later that day. Jessica almost felt guilty about getting the girl to begin work.

"Just coffee now. I'd like to take it on the patio. I'm going to be joined by a party of two a bit later."

"Very good then."

Lora led her through the empty space of the dining room, which had been so much livelier the previous night. Once settled in at the table on the patio that she had been seated at the morning before, Jessica looked around her; the empty patio confirmed that she was indeed the only early riser of her previous companions—or of any other guest for that matter. Soon the coffee arrived, and Jessica waited expectantly for Aspen and Thornes to appear as well. She hoped the caffeine would make her brain sharp enough to handle what would likely be an interesting negotiation between the three of them.

About thirty minutes later, Jessica stopped staring at her coffee cup as though trying to discern her future in the dark grinds at the bottom of the white china to notice two men approaching. She gauged they were heading in her direction. The man in front had to be Louis Aspen, the producer, and the other, the screenwriter. Of the two, the first was obviously in charge. He was striding forward as the other man trailed behind. Aspen appeared to be in his early forties, with short-cropped, blond hair without a hint of gray in it and a carefully trimmed mustache of the same flaxen color. Right behind him was, no doubt, Michael Thornes. He was a touch shorter, with darker hair parted on the side and of longer, artistic length. His bluntly cut locks had no curl to them and flopped onto the edges of his shirt collar as he walked along the patio's flagstones.

"Jessica, I'm Louis Aspen," the blond man said, reaching her table and confirming her guess had been spot-on. He didn't lean forward to shake her hand. "It's good to finally meet in person."

"Yes, it is." She also was sizing him up as she could see he was her.

"I'm happy that you took me up on my offer to come to Castle Ryan for these discussions. Only the tiny, least optimistic part of me thought you might not actually show; the bigger part was positive that you would."

"I wouldn't have stood you up."

"No? Well, that's encouraging. I hope your stay has been pleasant so far. Have you been satisfied with the place while waiting for us to get here? We wanted to give you a day to relax on your own."

"Yes. It's been fine. I've been very comfortable. Thank you for asking."

"Good. Good. And this is Michael Thornes, the screenwriter I mentioned to you." He turned behind him and grabbed the other man's arm, pulling him toward him as way of introduction.

"Please sit down, both of you," Jessica said, assuming since she had beat them to the table that morning it was her role to play hostess.

"Thank you." The two men each grabbed chairs across from her. "Michael's very excited by the project's concept. Aren't you, Michael? I could barely keep him under control." He laughed quietly at his own joke.

"Yes, I am," Michael agreed, not seeming to mind his partner's manner. "I have some ideas I'd like to hash out as soon as possible."

"Michael has worked on several projects with me before. So he feels he can rush ahead and skip over the preliminaries. But Jessica hasn't, so she may need to go a little slower. Isn't that right, Jessica? We don't want to frighten her so she scurries away. Now do we?"

"Exactly."

"I thought so."

"We spoke so briefly before I left home. But now that we're all together, I hadn't really asked how you came to know so much about the *situations* I've found myself in recently."

"Didn't we discuss that already? I thought we did. Oh well. Let's go into more detail about that now."

"I think that would be helpful."

"Of course. Why it was Tom Martine, your friend, the journalist, who was so instrumental in engaging you and Inspector Raynaud on your last *caper,* should I say. He mentioned to me how you and that Canadian narcotics detective have ended up solving three—" He turned to his partner. "Think of it, Michael. Three murders!" Michael provided the expected nod of his head. "Tom was quite effusive about your investigative successes," Aspen concluded.

"Oh, Tom Martine, of course!" Jessica said. "I knew you learned something of my history from Tom, but I guess I didn't realize just how much!"

Why hadn't Jessica figured out that was the strongest and probably only connection for Thornes to be so interested in her? Tom had just recently inveigled her to go to Paris. He had wanted her to gain access to an art museum owned by a French industrialist he thought might be putting profits over best practices in a genetics lab he also owned and Tom's sister, Lucy, had relied on. That Alain's daughter, Odette, was interning at the museum had been Tom's entry card for Jessica and Alain to help him gain financial information about the Frenchman's corporation. The case had lethal complications that nearly cost Jessica her own life. So it was with additional trepidation that she listened to what Thornes was now saying to her.

"Yes. Tom wrote a brief but excellent piece on a project I collaborated on not that long ago. So when we ran into each other and grabbed a beer together, he ended up spilling the beans about some of your recent exploits. That's when I got the idea that I was just the man to bring them to a mass audience."

"Oh, I see."

"Jessica, you shouldn't hide your brilliant light under a barrel, you know! Anyway, have you thought about your *pitch?*"

"My *pitch?* I'm not sure I understand."

"Well, I guess that means that you haven't." Aspen chuckled to himself. "Not to worry. Not to worry. Michael and I had enough time to go over things before we arrived. Why don't we discuss our ideas and see how they appeal to you? We would, of course, very much like to get your friend, Raynaud, in on this as well. Of course, that would be expected."

"Alain?"

"Yes. We figured we'd start by talking just with you at this time. But we'd want him in on this also, as soon as possible, of course."

"Alain." Jessica involuntarily rubbed the back of her neck.

"Yes. You must have realized that."

Jessica picked up her coffee cup and took a good, long swig of the strong, dark liquid. But it went down the wrong way so that she had to follow it with a glass of cold water to stop from choking uncontrollably. She had half expected either one of the creative team to say something just like that. But not so quickly. *Not just yet.* Now that Louis had mentioned Alain, the reality of potential next steps overwhelmed her. "You would like him to come over to Ireland to discuss this with you both? I guess it makes sense you would."

"Yes. Of course, we do. But we can hold off on that for just a bit while we get the preliminaries out of the way. That would be all right. Michael, why don't you start by outlining what you've been thinking about the project?"

Michael took only a moment to brush away Lora, who had just brought more coffee to the table, before he launched into a detailed summary of some of his ideas. This went on for a good hour as he got more and more animated, advancing his ideas and barely giving Jessica a chance to take in each one before the next one arrived. He concluded with "I envision five or six episodes, serializing Jessica and Alain's recent murder investigations."

Jessica quickly realized he had omitted any mention at all of the substantial financial backing that would most likely be needed for the project. It seemed to be a glaring omission, and she suddenly wondered if the purpose of this project was to touch her for a sizable sum.

Louis broke in, as though reading her mind. "And don't worry about the financials. I've got all my investors lined up already. One of them—he's a musician; that's all I'm allowed to say—is especially interested in the project. His only stipulation is that the locale for all the episodes be in Ireland. He's also heard about the history of this particular castle and the locals' preoccupation with *the ghost of Evelyn*." He wiggled his fingers on either side of his head like a Halloween trickster at an open door while he said the last four words. "So if we can check off both boxes with the same project, that would be smashing!"

"So you've heard about that legend?" Jessica asked cautiously. She was in no way willing to share what she, Frankie, and Stanley debated in the early morning hours after Frankie's frightening experience.

"Oh yes. We—Michael and I—feel it will add *spiritual caché* to help guarantee the project a total success, not to mention the fact that working her story into at least one episode is a major stipulation of one of our most generous investors."

Jessica looked back and forth between the two enthusiastic faces staring at her from across the table, and then she said, "Well, obviously I need to think long and hard about all that you've both discussed."

"Of course," Louis said.

"It's a tempting proposition. But I think you'll both agree it requires a good deal of thought."

"Definitely, definitely, but don't wait *too* long. Not too long. No."

"I won't."

"You know we're very eager to move forward and get started with all the gears in the right place. And the sooner we can get your buy-in, the sooner we can make plans to approach Inspector Raynaud as well!"

"I don't envision that being an easy task to accomplish—even if I do *buy in*."

"We wouldn't expect that, but we still have total confidence in your abilities, don't we, Michael?" Louis looked at his partner in the project for confirmation and, once obtained with a small up-and-down shake of the head, continued speaking. "Now you ponder all that we've discussed this morning. And let's plan on getting together tomorrow for further discussion. Does that work for you?"

Jessica found herself nodding in unison with their bobbing heads, although at the back of her own mind, she knew she was reaching the point of no return.

Eight
A Ride to Town

"Is there a car I may use to get to Dalkey?" Jessica asked. She had left Aspen and Thornes and found Brenda once again behind the large reception desk in the main hall of the castle.

"Why, yes," Brenda answered. "We keep an old car out by the gardening shed for the guests to use from time to time. It's small, but it does service nicely. I think it'll work for you. Let me ring up Alvin Hill and have him meet you at the shed and give you the keys. Now are you comfortable driving by yourself? You do remember that we drive on the other side of the road, don't you? I wouldn't want you to have an accident."

"Yes, I remember. I think I can manage all right if I take it slow."

Jessica left the castle by a side door after the proprietress mapped out how to find the head gardener on the property, and it didn't take long for her to locate the spot. The shed was a large, wooden building with vertical wood siding that had weathered the many years it must have stood there. There were patches of thick, green moss on the shadier side of the building; they looked like they could be scraped off with a large spoon from the underlying brown wood. But the shed seemed to be in fairly good repair, without signs of rotting. And Jessica hoped that boded well for the condition of the car she was to borrow. She would need it to be in good shape because she would be navigating roads that were still unfamiliar to her. She had no wish to be stranded by herself on one of them in a broken-down car.

Standing to the side of the shed stood an older man. He was bald on the top of his head but had a shock of white hair, which bordered the bald area above it in a semicircle. He also had a thick, walrus mustache that covered and almost curled around the edges of his lips. He was wearing loose, dark-green trousers. The trousers were tucked into high, rubber boots, which had deep stains, likely accumulated over years of wear while tramping through piles of damp earth and fallen leaves. A good quantity of the local sod was crusted onto them, and from the expression on Alvin's face, it was clear he wouldn't think to remove even a speck of the solid muck before transferring a loaner car to any Castle Ryan guest.

"Are you Dr. Shepard then?" he asked as Jessica came over to him.

She could see him looking her over as if she were a new colt that needed breaking in. It made her think of an old Western movie in which the greenhorn is shown a gentle-appearing horse only to have it violently buck and throw as soon as it is ridden by the invading upstart. But from what Brenda had intimated, Jessica knew it was more probable the car Alvin would provide was likely to go too slow than too fast.

So she just said, "Yes. Brenda said you would set me up in a car so I can drive to town."

"Will do. Will do. Come with me." His comments, though brief, seemed friendlier than his appearance. He led her along the side of the shed to where a small, black car was waiting for her. It looked innocuous enough. He started to hand her the car keys. But then he hesitated, holding them back in his hands, which struck her as a good deal stronger than expected from the other physical signs of his age. "You do know to drive on the left side of the road?"

With the same bravado she had displayed to Brenda, she carefully omitted the fact that this would be her first time doing it. "Of course," she said a bit too loudly, hearing her own words resonate through her head. She cleared her throat and continued silently rationalizing. After all, the road down from the castle was so narrow that it probably wouldn't make much difference which side of the road she was on. And she bravely remembered the phrase "See one. Do one. Teach one" that had been hammered into her during her early medical training.

Alvin looked at her skeptically. But then he finally placed the car keys in her outstretched palm, and Jessica quickly closed a fist around them before he could change his mind. The weight of the keys in her hand somehow reassured her and gave her renewed confidence to match her false bravado.

"Just lock her up when you come back, and leave the keys in the inn," he said. "I'll likely be working the grounds so I'll not be here to accept them when you get back. Good day to you."

Jessica wondered if he was really thinking *if* you get back. But she pushed that thought to the far recesses of her mind, behind her resurgent confidence. "I'll do that. Thank you."

He turned away and went into the wooden shed without speaking another word to her, although she could swear that she heard him muttering softly to himself.

Jessica pulled on the handle of the car door. It stuck like glue. But bracing her spine against the car's side, and with good, old-fashioned elbow grease, she finally managed to pull the door open. It made a loud thud as it flew back, extended into its full open angle, and she almost flew back onto her own haunches as well. She righted herself and gave a quick, satisfied jerk of her chin—there was no way she would have called back Alvin to her rescue to get the door open—and she got inside.

One look at the controls told her the car didn't have a GPS system. "Damn!" She pulled out her cell phone and was happy to see she had enough reception to let the phone lead her down the hill and to Millie's coffee shop. That was her destination. She started the engine and, after she could hear the reassuring *put-put* of the engine, drove past the front of the castle, out of the grounds, and back toward Dalkey.

She felt herself slowly getting the hang of sitting on the right side of the car and driving on the left side of the road. As she maneuvered the car along, she also asked herself if her current plan made sense. Aspen and Thornes's ideas were still fresh in her mind, and she weighed their pluses and minuses; she kept summing them up to try to come to a solution. *Should she go along with them?* The sticking point was whether or not she—and Alain—should give up their cherished anonymity. So the verdict—at least on her part—tottered between a yes and a no. As an answer hadn't miraculously presented itself earlier, she had decided it was best to do some sleuthing on her own—about the other question that was still disturbing her peace of mind.

Frankie's possible spectral visitation in the early morning hours, as well as Aspen and Thornes's knowledge of Castle Ryan's ghost story, intrigued Jessica. She needed to sound the problem out with another living person. She just couldn't let it go. It was consuming her with as much force as her uncertainty over whether to agree to the television project. But she was uncomfortable approaching any of the Ryans about her conundrum; they might be reluctant to discuss the more unsavory history of the castle they currently owned. That wouldn't be unexpected. And besides, her tentative overture to Bevin Ryan hadn't garnered any fruit.

No. Jessica felt the best source to start with was Millie, and it was her coffee shop where Jessica first heard the tale from Millie and Sean. It was likely that Millie, who displayed such indignation at not being taken seriously, would be eager to share any tales she had with a sympathetic ear. Jessica just couldn't appear skeptical, as Sean had; if she did, Millie would likely turn from raconteur and show the irritation she had displayed when doubted. So here Jessica was, driving with only some residual trepidation the borrowed car, which was lent to her with the graciousness of the castle's proprietors, and heading back down the hill to sound Millie out in the woman's own caffeine-laced haunt.

Jessica followed the auditory directions that were pronounced with digital precision by her cell phone's robotic voice. Luckily there were only a few spots where she momentarily lost the GPS connection; for those, she used her best directional sense to continue on the right path. Finally, after what seemed to be twice the time it had taken Sean to get her up to the castle, she gave a deep sigh of relief when she realized she had made it back down to town. She quickly spotted Millie's shop. She found a parking space not too far away from it, locked the car, and pocketed the car keys carefully into her purse. The last thing she wanted to do was to lose the keys and have to call up Alvin Hill for a spare pair.

As she entered the shop, Jessica noted the absence of customers. Her shoes echoed against the wooden floorboards of the empty store. She almost smacked herself for not calling ahead to make sure she would find Millie inside. But then she saw Millie bent over behind the counter. The girl was arranging some lower shelves that held clean, white mugs for coffee. Millie got up from her squatting position, and Jessica hoped she still recognized her as the recently arrived American tourist whom Sean had taken under his wing. Now Jessica was on her own, but she had a feeling that she might actually be in better standing that way. Without Sean's jocularity to get under Millie's thin skin, Jessica might make greater headway. She went up to Millie and smiled as sweetly as she could.

"Millie?" Jessica asked.

"Yes?"

"I don't know if you remember me, but I was in your shop the other day. Your friend Sean gave me a lift up to Castle Ryan. I was here for a few minutes while he changed his clothes."

"Yes?" A frown crinkled Millie's forehead. Jessica wasn't sure whether it was from annoyance at her feeble attempt to ingratiate herself with the shopkeeper before getting to her point or an attempt on Millie's part to place Jessica's face in memory.

"I was listening to you and Sean talking about the castle," Jessica continued.

"Don't worry. I remember you, and I remember the conversation, all right. Sean likes to get my goat. But that's fine. I don't mind as much as I put on. We're old friends so we can talk to each other that way. It doesn't mean anything. Look, I hope you didn't take it too seriously. It wasn't anything that you did wrong." Millie's expression lightened up a bit when she said this.

"Well, I couldn't help hearing what you said about the ghost."

"*Oh.*" Millie rolled the word slowly out of her mouth, as if she were a singer practicing her vowels during vocal warm-up exercises. "Oh, I see. So you heard *that part* of our little talk. So you're *not* a skeptic, like my smart little friend Sean, now are you? Well, I'm happy about that, at least."

"A skeptic? *No.* Not really. You see, let me explain. A few others have mentioned something about the legend—"

"Legend?" Millie raised one eyebrow up to the top of her blonde head. The eyebrows, at least, hadn't been frosted pink. So the gesture was more effective than it would have been otherwise.

Jessica racked her brain for a less confrontational, descriptive noun. *"Story?"*

"That's better! I don't like the word *legend*. I consider it insulting to history. But I won't hold it against you. You're new here so you shouldn't be expected to know any better. Friends then?"

"Friends definitely!"

"Good. So what do you want to know?"

Millie looked around her shop as if to confirm that it was still empty. Then she leaned her elbows on the counter, unaware that in her eagerness to converse with Jessica she performed the very act that she had scolded Sean about the other day. But she failed to notice Jessica observing her and waited expectantly for Jessica's answer. It was clear Millie was eager to indulge her creative, storytelling side to the greatest extent by indulging this tourist as long as it didn't negatively impact the accounts receivable column in her own ledger book.

"All I know," Jessica said, "is what I've heard so far: that there was a woman named Evelyn who lived in the castle many years ago, that she wanted more than her husband and I guess society at the time—was able to give her while she indulged her writing skills, and that she died and it wasn't clear how or why."

"Oh, it was *clear* all right! At least, that's what my gram tells me. *Her* mother told her about it and, I think, used it as a moral tale to keep Gram in her safe, little place. Things were different then, weren't they? It's a damn shame! That's all I can say!"

"What did your gram tell you?"

"Are you really interested? You're not just pulling my leg?

Heh, has Sean put you up to this?" Millie narrowed her eyes slightly as she studied Jessica's face for clues.

"No, not at all. *He hasn't!* Of course, I'm truly interested in the whole story."

"Well. All right then. Let's go talk to her then."

"Your grandmother you mean? You'll take me to see your grandmother?"

"Sure. Who else would I be talking about? Why not? Look around you." Millie spread the palm of her hand in a sweeping motion from left to right above the coffee counter, and she indicated the empty space around her. "Do you see anyone in the shop now who would miss me for a while?"

"Well, no."

"Exactly! So there's no problem at all. Do you have a car that we can use? Mine's not working too reliably lately. I wouldn't want us to get broken down on the way."

"Well, yes. As a matter of fact, I do." *Good thinking*, Jessica thought.

"Great. Then you can drive, and I'll direct. It's a very short trip. Don't worry!"

"Where are we going?"

"Killiney!"

Nine
To Killiney

Millie closed the shop just as two elderly women, walking arm in arm, arrived. Jessica recognized them as the same ones she saw drinking tea together on her first day in Dalkey.

Millie turned back to them and said, "I'm sorry, but I can't let you in now, ladies. We're off to see my gram. I'll open up the store again when I get back from visiting her."

"That's fine, dear," they said in unison. Then the taller one said, "June and I will just go and do our shopping, and we'll hold off on our tea until you return."

"That's right, Iris," said June. "Now isn't that nice that you're going to spend some time with your grandmother? Family is so important. Be sure and give her our regards. You have a lovely day for a short hop to Killiney."

As they conversed, the two ladies studied Jessica closely, and despite their advanced years, it was clear their minds were sharp. They remembered her as the American who had needed the ride to Castle Ryan the day before.

"So you're also bringing your grandmother a visitor," Iris said, looking directly at Jessica while trying valiantly to obtain additional information from Millie.

"That's right," Millie answered firmly, pursing her lips in annoyance at being detained by the pair. "We shouldn't be long. I'll have your teas waiting for you both when we come back. Don't worry about that."

"Now isn't that nice?" Iris repeated, obviously finally realizing that she wasn't going to get any further enlightening conversation out of Millie. The two women reluctantly waddled off, still arm in arm, each with a mesh shopping bag hanging from their outside elbows; they were like two little soldiers ready to do battle in the small shops lining the main thoroughfare of the town.

"The McLeish sisters," Millie said in explanation. "They're total characters and the biggest gossips in town. But I know how to handle them. Of course, they also know if I don't answer their questions, I'll have to undercharge them for the tea." Millie added that tidbit as she got into the car next to Jessica. She shook her head in exasperation, but from the sound of her voice, she had recovered some of her good humor at the thought of the jaunt to Killiney. "They have their tea almost every day in my shop. It's what keeps them going. But I guess they help me to pay the rent and the utilities and stay in business. So I should accept that I'm lucky they find it a good place to watch the world go by." She scratched the top of her head as though perplexed by her own good fortune.

"I met someone who does the same thing every day at the castle," Jessica said, glancing at Millie. Soon it was clear Millie was on the same page.

"Oh. I know what you're getting at. You must be talking about Amy Stanwich. Yes. She's another one of their type, all right."

"That's exactly right. How did you know so easily who I was talking about?"

"It just makes sense, I guess. That's the only reason I thought of Amy. Nothing more. Her cottage abuts the grounds of Castle Ryan. Although if it were me, I wouldn't want to be reminded about having to sell out my land by sitting there and looking at it every day of my life. What's gone is gone. That's what I say." She continued to watch the road in front of them.

"Did Amy have to do it then? Sell, I mean."

"I don't know all the fine details, but I think that was the case. At least from what I've heard tell about it. *Hey! Watch out! Left side of the road! Left side of the road!*" Millie screeched out the commands while she clutched both sides of her seat and jammed both her feet down firmly onto the floor of the car. *"You don't want to get us killed, do you?"*

Jessica had almost nicked a car heading too quickly for her own comfort in the opposite direction. She immediately decided it was time to hold off on any further conversation except to listen to Millie's now totally focused directions to get them safely out of Dalkey. No, she certainly didn't want to get them killed. But it was also clear Millie wasn't going to be taking any further chances by entrusting her health and safety to this American driver without watching like a hawk, not only the road ahead of them, but also her companion's every vehicular move.

Killiney was south of Dalkey, overlooking Dublin Bay, and Jessica was just as happy after their near run-in to let Millie guide her there. They seemed to be getting closer to the sea as they drove along, and despite the nearness of the two towns, Jessica could feel a change in air through the open car windows as they drove. The road they were on was less congested than that of the other town. And Jessica was grateful there were no further incidents with any other cars in their way. She knew if there were another episode, Millie would demand they stop the car and switch seats so that she could drive instead. Something inside Jessica didn't want that potential occurrence to somehow make it back to Alvin Hill. If it did, she could almost visualize the gardener's self-satisfied smirk when he got wind of it through the local gossip chain.

Jessica studiously continued to watch the road as Millie directed. And soon they reached a group of small, tidy homes that made up the neighborhood in which Millie's grandmother lived.

"Now remember Gram is well into her nineties. But I'm telling you that she still has a very clear brain. She has a nurse— Mrs. Robson—to care for her. But I don't think you'll have any trouble extracting from Gram whatever details you'd like to know about Evelyn and the castle in general. The McLeish sisters and Amy Stanwich may have their *tea and questions* to keep them going, but Gram has her *stories* to do it for her. Yes, that's what keeps *her* going. By the way, what's your name? I never thought to ask you, and Gram won't like it if you're not introduced to her properly. She keeps to the old ways in that sense."

"Jessica Shepard. But Jessica's fine."

"Got it."

Jessica stopped the car in front of the house. And she and Millie went up the path to the front door. Millie rang the bell, and the *ding-dong* seemed barely loud enough to elicit any response from inside. But a few minutes later, the door was opened by the nurse who introduced herself as Mrs. Robson. To Jessica she had every appearance of an efficient caregiver. She looked to be in her fifties, and was one, Jessica expected, well able to deal with a nonagenarian—even one with a clear intellect as Millie had described her grandmother as having. Mrs. Robson had short, gray hair unlikely to require unnecessary effort to get her locks into perfect place before her duty hours. And she was wearing a spotless white shirt, knee-length, dark skirt, and sensible black shoes, all of which served as her uniform for the day.

"Well, hello, Millie," she said, clearly indicating that Millie's unexpected visits were treats. "So you're here to see Gram today. She'll be so pleased to see you. This isn't your day to visit. What a nice surprise this will be for her!"

"How is she doing, Mrs. Robson? Well today, is she?"

"Oh. Very well today. Very well indeed. You picked just the right day to drop by to see her. She's at her best today."

Millie flashed a triumphant smile at Jessica. "You see, we chose a good day to come by. That'll be helpful." She turned back to Mrs. Robson. "I've brought a guest with me. She's an American. She wants to talk to Gram. I've been telling her about some of Gram's stories from long ago. And she wants to hear them direct from the horse's mouth. I thought the best thing was to bring her right over."

"Your grandmother will be so happy to hear that. She's quite the storyteller she is, as you know only too well. Why don't you two come in and see her? She's in the kitchen now, and there's more than enough room for you all to sit in there comfortably. It's a nice, big, old-fashioned kitchen. That's why we spend so much of our time in there. Doesn't look it from the front of the house, but it is. I was just going to put up a pot of tea for only the two of us. But I'll make it for four, and a little stronger than usual, and we'll have a nice little tea party. Why don't we? Come inside. Please."

Jessica and Millie followed Mrs. Robson through the tidy house and into the kitchen in the back. The room had a large window to one side of it; the window was half covered by a short-ruffled, white-lace curtain on the top of it. The window looked out onto a small, back garden. Jessica could just make out through the window some red rose bushes bordering both sides of a small plot of green grass. In contrast to the old-world style of the window curtains, the cheery room was lined around its perimeter with an abundance of modern kitchen appliances, which sparkled as if they were being constantly cleaned.

Millie's grandmother was seated at a long, rectangular wooden table in the center of the room. She was patiently waiting for her nurse to come back from answering the front door. Mrs. Robson was perfectly correct. The size of the table and the room itself would easily accommodate all of them while they drank tea together. Millie's grandmother watched them come over closer to her.

The nonagenarian was a sturdy woman, and her appearance seemed to belie her age. Thick, white hair framed a face that sheltered bright, blue eyes that still expressed an intelligence that had likely been honed by life's varied experiences. Jessica knew with one look at her that whatever history this woman related would be accurate, although it might be sprinkled with some local color to boot.

"Hello, Gram," Millie said. She bent down to plant a gentle kiss on the elderly woman's wrinkled face, who in turn raised her right hand to caress her granddaughter's cheek. The pink, frosted ends of Millie's hair stood out in vibrant relief against the stark white of her grandmother's head. And for a moment, all Jessica could think of was a white-coated, baby bunny rabbit with underlying pink skin. The contrasting colors were exactly the same, and all that was missing was a little rabbit's black nose. "I've brought a guest, Gram. This is Jessica Shepard. She's come to have tea with us. I've been telling her some of your stories. She's very interested in them."

"Hello, Jessica," the old woman said, smiling at her new guest. She appeared genuinely pleased; there wasn't a hint of irritation at being interrupted at her scheduled teatime. It would seem that a visitor was a treat worth a delay in her ritual.

"Hello," Jessica began.

"Now just call me *Gram*. Everyone else does at this point in my life so that I've practically forgotten my own true name. But it's Rose, if you care to remember it. I guess no one told you that yet."

"I will call you Gram as you wish, but Rose is such a pretty name."

"So is Jessica, my dear."

Mrs. Robson was standing with her back to them, facing the stove and busily working on the tea things as Jessica and Millie sat down with Rose. A few minutes later, the nurse positioned a white china pot with a thin, gold, swirled pattern running diagonally about its sides, filled with fragrant tea, on a place mat in the center of the table. It was soon accompanied by cups of sugar and milk, and a cup, saucer, and petite teaspoon were placed in front of each of them. Mrs. Robson then sat down with the three others, obviously eager to hear the details of Rose's stories.

"So Gram, Jessica has been hearing talk about the history of the castle and that of Evelyn," Millie said. "I told her you could give her the story as close to it as anyone around here."

"Yes. That's right. I certainly can." She visibly brightened even more, likely realizing this would be an extended visit, and one in which she would be providing the entertainment. "It's not a small matter of pride to me than I can. Many is a time my mother used to tell me the story, but never at bedtime, mind you. She would *never* do that.

"Now let me see, my mother would have been about ten years old when it all happened. Bailey Lansing—that was his name—he was the owner of all the land around what's now the Castle Ryan estate. And he built that castle for his new wife, Evelyn. That was her name. Oh, there were some old ruins there at the time of the building, but he built a brand-new castle for her on the site after he had everything else trundled off. No respect for history, that one." She harrumphed. "He was some type of industrialist and made all kinds of money. It was easier at that time to do that—at least for some, that is. And he *poured* his money hand over fist into his new home. The locals thought he was crazy spending so much money like he did. But they were very glad of the work it provided for most of the families around here. I can tell you that much. Things were tight then—for most of the people anyway. Well, Bailey thought that his bride would pass her time taking care of his house—oh, he was very proud of what he had built—and that she'd entertain, and she'd give him many children to carry on his name and all that."

Rose took a sip of tea, heightening the suspense with some delay, before carefully placing the cup back down on the table and continuing. "Now Bailey knew Evelyn liked to write stories and poems and things like that, but he thought that just showed she was smart and worthy of him. I guess he thought she'd just do it as a pastime—something to pass the long winter nights. Guess he wasn't the type to keep her warm himself." She laughed at her own joke. "But she turned out to be a serious *writer*. And she wanted to *publish* her work—and under her *own* name. This was the thing my mother said infuriated Bailey. You see, my grandmother did some work at the house, so the kitchen gossip would leave the castle and come back to my mother's home that way. Anyway, like I said, my mother told me that Evelyn wanted to publish under her own name."

She leaned over closer to Jessica and Millie in confidence, and after throwing a quick wink to Mrs. Robson, she whispered, "There was some who thought she was a little *taken* with her potential publisher, and he with her. Anyway, she died before she could publish much of anything. More's the pity." Rose took one more swallow of tea, as if in reward for a job well done.

"How did she die?" Jessica blurted out, too loudly for social niceties by the look she read on Mrs. Robson's face. But Jessica was totally enthralled by the elderly woman's ability to spin a good tale, and she was finding it difficult to control her enthusiasm and maintain her composure during the tea ritual.

But Rose didn't seem upset by Jessica's question. "Now if you could answer *that* question, you'd be famous around here—at least among some of us—like Mrs. Robson and me, who like to remember our history—good or bad. Don't we, Martha?" She didn't wait for a reply from her caregiver but went on with her tale. "My mother told me that Evelyn was found on the grounds, just behind the castle. And she was dead by the time they found her. My mother would not tell me anymore. No, she wouldn't, no matter how hard I pressed her."

Rose looked around her at the three faces she had managed to totally transfix with her story, and she gave a soft chuckle. Then she turned again to Mrs. Robson. "I guess I still can tell a story with the best of them, can't I, Martha? Maybe I should take up *writing* myself? What do you say? Do you think that's a grand idea?"

Martha Robson smiled warmly at her patient and said, "That's only too true, Gram. Maybe I can be your secretary. Will you hire me for that if writing becomes your new profession?"

Rose chuckled again, obviously pleased with how successful a raconteur she was considered by her audience.

But Jessica was silent; she was falling into a deep study. She couldn't help thinking back to Castle Ryan's outdoor patio, where she had lunched and where she had met with Aspen and Thornes to discuss their project ideas. That must have been the very spot where Evelyn's body had been discovered all those years ago. She wondered if she'd ever think of the spot in the very same way; it must have been where, so many years ago, Evelyn Lansing had taken her last gasp of dying breath.

"Oh, but you're not drinking your tea!" Rose suddenly said. "Martha, I feel guilty. I've not been a very good hostess, now have I? Think of me going on and on like that. And my guest not drinking her tea while it's still hot! That's a *crime!*"

"No. No. Don't think that," Jessica said, finally realizing she had mentally left the convivial social gathering and, totally missing the mischievous smile on Rose's lips, took a deep swig of the fragrant liquid. It was still surprisingly tasty and pungent, despite its having cooled to a tepid temperature while she was so engrossed in the elderly woman's story.

"Gram, if you came to my shop now and then, I'd probably sell more tea and coffee than I do now. My patrons would keep ordering more and more just to stay and hear all your many tales. We could bring you in like storytelling time at the library. Now that is a grand idea!"

"That's a very sweet thought. You're a good granddaughter, Millie, and I love you."

"Me too, Gram." Millie smiled broadly at her grandmother, and then she turned back to Jessica. "Jessica, if you've heard enough for today, speaking of my shop, I'd best be getting back. There are probably at least two fine ladies waiting to get in for their daily tea. The McLeish sisters, Gram," she added in explanation. "We kept them waiting so we could drop by. They should be finished with their shopping by now." She looked down at her watch and confirmed the necessity to return to town.

Martha said, "You mustn't keep those two waiting any longer. I'll let you out." She got up from the table and led Jessica and Millie back out to the front door.

"Thank you both so much for coming to see her. It makes her day, you know. Her happiness from this visit will last the entire week!"

Ten
The Music of Romance

essica returned to Castle Ryan with her head still swirling from Rose's story. She had left Millie at her coffee shop in town. As predicted, the two elderly women, whom Jessica now knew quite well to be the McLeish sisters, had been waiting impatiently outside the shop. Each had been practically tapping her toes against the pavement until the doors were reopened, eager to get on with their tea after a satisfactory shopping trip. Their mesh bags were filled with the savory items they had purchased for the week. Jessica then drove back to the castle without any accident and returned the car to its allotted spot outside the gardening shed, content that there was no dent on the vehicle and Alvin Hill need not survey it for damage.

Jessica went up to the empty reception desk. It was the time of day when it was unlikely for new guests to be arriving or for old ones to be departing the castle. She deposited the car keys in the slotted container that was marked for their return just as the gardener had instructed. But as she turned away to head up the staircase to her room, she heard the mournful strains of a piano being played in a minor key. Although clearly audible, the sound seemed to be coming from some distance. She remembered Alice mentioned while seating her for lunch on the patio that Stanley Bogart sometimes played a baby grand piano outside the castle's conference room. Jessica decided she wanted to see the pianist in action. And since it seemed as though this was a time he wasn't sequestered in his room, studying his biographies of great composers, it was as good a time as any to try to do so.

Jessica followed the strains of music floating in the air. She headed down a long corridor. It led to a set of carpeted stairs, which turned around on itself to a lower level that was directly beneath the entrance hall. The soft carpeting muffled the sound of her footsteps as she moved closer and closer to the origin of the musical notes; they resonated through the depths of the underground passage and led out to the expanse of the lower level of the castle.

There she saw Stanley, seated on a piano bench, his back toward her. He was positioned stiffy in front of the black piano and didn't notice her as she came toward him. He continued emotionally pulling the notes out of the large instrument with a force that was surprising for someone who had otherwise seemed so tentative. His fingers flew back and forth over the keys with total abandon. When Jessica practically hovered over him, and her shadow darkened the white keys of the keyboard, he finally looked up from it and noticed her.

"What you're playing, is it yours or someone else's?" Jessica asked.

"The music?"

"Yes." Jessica still stood over him. "May I sit down?"

"Of course." He slid over to the edge of the piano bench to make room for her to join him. He was wearing a T-shirt and jeans. It was a garb she hadn't yet seen him wear. He suddenly looked much younger than he had before from their prior encounters on the patio, at dinner, or even on the landing outside Frankie's door when the writer had *seen* Evelyn Lansing's apparition. "Yes. It's mine, but I'm still working on it. I haven't yet gotten it down exactly the way I want it."

"It's very beautiful, but it's a little sad."

"I know. I've been trying to lighten it up a bit. But it just seems to keep coming back to how I originally wrote it. I'm not sure why. I've been sitting here working on the piece and trying to figure that out."

"Maybe your fingers are *hearing* how you're feeling?"

"Probably that's it. But I didn't want to admit it to myself. It's such a cliché to say one needs to suffer to put enough emotion into a musical piece to make it great. It just sounds so much like an old romantic movie."

"Well, I like old romantic movies, but are you having romantic troubles?"

"Is it so obvious?"

"Well, yes. It is, actually."

Stanley looked down at his hands, which were now both dangling over the piano keys. His fingernails were neatly clipped. Jessica remembered something else Alice had remarked about the pianist—that he had extremely long fingers. They were very long. Jessica imagined they would allow him to easily span over an octave on the keyboard. He noticed her looking at his hands, because self-consciously he soon clasped them together on his lap. Then he said, "It's hard when one's advances are constantly rebuffed. I guess I'm just funneling my disappointment into my music. That's healthy, isn't it?"

He looked so earnestly at Jessica that she knew there was absolutely no sarcasm in the question he was posing; he seemed to be seeking confirmation of the success of his attempt at self-healing. So she decided to give him just that.

She said very slowly, "I think so, as long as you don't let it stop you from seeing the world around you in a better light." She waited a minute for her words to sink in. Then she said, "You know what? Why don't you play something else for me now? I'd really like to hear you play something else. Something a little brighter? How about that?"

He suddenly laughed. A grin, which she could almost describe as devilish, broke out across his face, and he started playing a jaunty Irish air. "Better? What do you think?"

"Much better! I like it! Why don't you play that for a while?"

Stanley played another air and then another. He seemed to begin to fail to notice her as he fell deeper and deeper into the magic spell of the happier music. Jessica figured she had done enough psychotherapy for the day, and quietly slid off the piano bench, leaving him to finish his piece in peace.

****

That night Castle Ryan was hosting a banquet in the main dining room. It was to be accompanied by live music to be provided by a group of local, Irish musicians. Jessica asked Brenda about the performers and was told she would hear harp, guitar, fiddle, flute, and bodhrán drum making up the quintet that would be entertaining the guests for the festivities. She was also advised to wear a formal cocktail dress because guests who attended the castle's parties tended to dress formally. *Glam* was to be the word of the night.

Now alone in her room, Jessica surveyed the few clothes she had put away in the large armoire on her arrival to Castle Ryan. The items dangling from cushioned, black, sateen hangers looked pitifully sparse in the depths of the capacious wardrobe. But she gave a sigh of relief when her eyes fell upon the black, spaghetti-strap, satin sheath she had thought to pack when she left home. Its length struck midcalf and would flow out gracefully about her slim limbs. The dress was sure to fit the bill as appropriate for the glamorous affair. A pair of black, patent leather sandals on her feet, and her favorite gold and moonstone parure in her ears and around her neck, would surely add a needed splash of elegance to the simple staple of an evening dress.

She left her room, closing the door behind her. She turned around and headed down the corridor, looking into her black, satin purse to check that she remembered to put a bright-red lipstick into its inner pouch. It was hard to see the black lipstick case against the black silk lining of the purse, but she could feel it lodged there. It had gotten caught up in one of the silk threads of the pouch, but she managed to extract it from the tangled threads and reinsert it so she could easily repair her lips throughout the night.

Relieved she hadn't forgotten it, she finally looked up, nearly bumping into Stanley, who was leaving his own room for the dinner dance. He no longer wore jeans and a T-shirt but was now dressed as a pianist might be for a formal evening. He wore a tuxedo with dress shirt and a plaid bow tie and cummerbund. The tuxedo jacket fit him well about the shoulders but was creased at the bottom flaps, as though he hadn't bothered to have it pressed after it was last pulled out for a performance before being packed hurriedly away. The bow tie, though, was fresh and expertly tied around his neck. Its precise, almost scientific arrangement made up for the defective state of the suit.

"You look ready for a performance," Jessica said encouragingly, hoping he was feeling more cheerful than he had been earlier.

"Yes. After dinner, the dancing will probably spill over from the dining room, where the quintet will play, and spread down to the conference room that they'll use as a ballroom for the night. At least, that's what's happened in the past when I've stayed here and they've had one of these events. I'm going to help out on the piano when the other musicians need to take a break."

"Well, I'm sure the Ryans will appreciate that. It sounds like it's sure to be a great evening. I can't wait for it to start."

"Have you seen Frankie? I wanted to ask her if she'll be sitting with me—*us* for the dinner. But I haven't seen her for a while."

"Did you knock on her door?" Jessica asked, pointing to the closed door to Frankie's room.

"I did, but there's no answer. I don't think she's in there."

"Maybe she finished dressing before us and is already downstairs. Maybe she couldn't wait for it to start either."

"I guess so. That makes sense."

"Well, why don't we go down and see if we can find her?"

Jessica led Stanley farther down the corridor. He hesitated for only a moment, and then, as though losing his own initiative, he dutifully followed her. As they passed the now infamous owl, she saw that, true to Brenda's initial conversation about the bird, it was formally outfitted for the evening as well. Joel or perhaps his sister, Alice, must have quietly dressed the bird while Jessica had been dressing. She marveled at the ability of the carpeting to have muffled any noise in the corridor because the owl had been totally bare when she had previously entered her room. She was sure of that. She hadn't heard any creaking like before, when she had been awakened by Frankie and Stanley in the early morning hours.

But now the bird was fully attired, and she had never heard a sound through her bedroom door. It wore on its prominent head a jaunty, red tam-o'-shanter with a black, fuzzy pom-pom in the center of the felt. It also wore a bow tie, similar to the one Stanley wore—*she hoped he didn't notice that*—and a black cape with a deep-red, satin lining. The cape was folded back over the broad wing of the bird, exposing the lining shockingly. It was the same color of blood, and it stopped Jessica in her tracks. Then she recovered, and she and Stanley passed the owl without either making a comment, as though silently agreeing to avoid the obvious impropriety of the Halloween-like trick on such an evening.

They turned the corridor's corner and headed toward the main staircase to descend to the cavernous hall below.

Louis Aspen and Michael Thornes will likely also be at the gala, Jessica suddenly thought. She hadn't seen either of them since their meeting that morning. They had seemed to disappear from the estate. They had been placed in rooms in the opposite wing of Castle Ryan and she hadn't bumped into them once during the day. She hadn't scouted out the other part of the castle and had no knowledge of what that wing was like, although Alice had said she preferred Jessica's side of the castle. Jessica imagined the other rooms were similar to the one that she, Stanley, and Frankie had been put in. Although perhaps the other rooms given to the producer and to the screenwriter were grander.

From what she could see of the corridor leading to the other wing, it did look to be part of the older section of the castle, just as Alice had described. Below the wallpaper, the wainscoting leading off in that direction was darker and more intricately carved. The passageway itself was also a little wider than the one leading to her room, suggesting the rooms on that side of the castle were likely to be larger as well.

Jessica and Stanley descended the last few steps of the broad staircase. They moved onto the center of the entrance hall and stood beneath the brilliant chandelier that sparkled above their heads. Jessica was surprised to see Amy Stanwich also standing there. Somehow it hadn't occurred to her that the older woman would present herself at Castle Ryan for anything other than her well-known afternoon teatime. But Amy was now grandly attired in formal dress. She was next to an elder man with a studious demeanor; he seemed like someone who didn't miss a detail as he watched Jessica and Stanley come over to their side.

Amy looked at her and said, "Jessica, dear, how lovely you look tonight. And you too, Mr. Bogart. I'm not excluding you from my compliment. Stanley, you are quite the gentleman."

"You're also looking very elegant this evening, Mrs. Stanwich," Jessica said.

"Amy, please!"

"Amy, then."

Amy had been transformed from *elderly country lady,* as outfitted in the suit Jessica had last seen her in, to a woman of regal significance. She was wearing a floor-length, lavender crêpe dress that adorned her bulky frame with a surprising degree of easy elegance. Around her neck was a glittering, black-stone choker that managed to surround the hefty bulk of its owner's neck without a struggle.

"Have you been introduced yet to Dr. Matthews? Dev is the man who keeps most of us alive and ticking around here. We would be truly lost without his services."

"No, I haven't met him," Jessica replied, turning toward the man who had his arm encircled by one of Amy's strong hands. Amy's fingers were encrusted with several black-stone rings that matched the stones about her neck.

"I'm merely the generalist around these parts, in way of explanation," Dr. Matthews said, smiling. "Amy just says that because she hasn't allowed me to raise my fees in over thirty years! So I have to keep working to pay the rent on my office, and my nurse's and receptionist's salaries."

"Well, that's also why you're so busy, Dev! Everyone in town relies on you. You are always too modest. That is your only failing." Amy patted his arm affectionately with her other hand. "But I'll sing his praises for him, if he won't. He sees to it that I'm able to sleep soundly, and that I don't end up in hospital. And for that I'm very grateful."

"Shall we go in?" the generalist asked meekly, obviously embarrassed by his grateful patient's paean.

"I think we should *wait* for Frankie," Stanley said, looking anxiously at his watch. "I thought she'd be here already, but she's obviously not. I don't know where she can be. I'm starting to get worried."

"Well, Stanley, I'm sure everything's fine. You should know that young ladies do like to make an entrance for these types of events. Why don't you wait here for Frankie? Then you can bring her in once she gets here. Dev can bring me and Jessica in. We'll save two spaces at a table for you and Frankie when you join us."

Jessica, with one arm on that of their escort, and Amy, with hers on the other, were led into the dining room. The space was even more grandly transformed than before. It would accommodate the many guests who were coming that evening, expecting to enjoy a long night of good food and lively music to entertain them. The room appeared even larger than it had the night before. The tables were arranged in a broad arc that encircled the shining floor; the middle area was left empty for the musicians to play and for the guests to dance during the first part of the evening, before descending to the ballroom for more enthusiastic dancing, as Stanley had told Jessica would occur.

The exit to the patio was left unencumbered so that the doors to the outside could be thrown open later in the evening;

that would allow a flow of diners, who didn't wish to dance, out toward the gardens to roam freely about the estate. The room would be filled with an enticing array of food—more varied than what was usually on the menu—so that the competing aromas from the tables would surely waft through the dining room and mingle with those of the fragrant flowers outside.

At the back edge of the dance floor, a long dais had been erected to allow the musicians to be easily seen above the heads of the guests who might dance to the music. The musicians were already in place. To the extreme left sat the first musician with a small harp on his lap. Next to him was the guitarist, then a man with a fiddle, then the flutist, and finally a man with a bodhrán drum on his thigh. They were a jovial quintet. Some had beards and some didn't. But all had longer hair than the common style, so they seemed to harken back to an earlier era as they joked among themselves and got their instruments tuned up for the night.

Jessica, Amy, and Dev found an empty table large enough to accommodate the group once Stanley would finally arrive with Frankie. Not long after the three settled in, Jessica saw Louis and Michael enter the dining room. That answered the question of whether or not the two would show. They were being escorted by the four Ryans: Bevin, in the lead, followed closely by his wife, Brenda, and their two grown children, Joel and Alice. The men wore tuxedos, and the women were in formal attire, like every other woman in the room. The fact that Louis and Michael were sharing the table with the Ryans clearly telegraphed their prominence among the evening's guests; it made Jessica think that it had the same significance as sharing the captain's table on a cruise liner.

As Jessica watched Brenda cautiously making her way through the dining room, tottering on stacked heels and attempting to hide the obvious unsteadiness of her right knee, she remembered Brenda mentioning she was also a patient of Dev Matthews. And Jessica wondered what the town's generalist thought about his other patient's conformity to style over his likely recommendations regarding the woman's bad knee.

"Dev, Brenda Ryan told me you've advised her to stay off her feet," Jessica said, turning to the other doctor at the table. "It looks like she'll not be doing that tonight." She pointed to Brenda, who had valiantly reached the table she was sharing with her family and her two exalted guests. Louis and Michael acknowledged Jessica with simultaneous nods of their heads as they sat down with the Ryans.

"I can only advise my patients," Matthews said. "I can't control them, as you must be all too aware. We are only here to *advise*, not to *dictate*."

"Don't listen to him, Jessica. Dev's a tyrant," Amy chimed in. "*To dictate is his motto.*"

"And you're much stronger than you make out, Amy!" the generalist countered. "I've known that for many years. You can't fool me."

Jessica listened to their back-and-forth with only half an ear because she was beginning to wonder when Stanley and Frankie would be joining them. She looked at her own watch, just as Stanley had done all those minutes before. Then she looked around the room.

Jessica could see that most of the other tables were by now filled with guests settling into their seats. The chairs were being pulled out and in and scraping across the highly polished floor. And the general conversation was creating a steady white noise throughout the large dining room. Only their table was sparsely inhabited, with the two place settings for the rest of their party still clearly unspoken for.

The musicians had finished tuning their instruments and began playing their initial selections for the evening. The music was lively but still constrained enough so that the guests could continue to converse with each other. The notes were floating through the air and competing with all the other sounds in the room. Later, the musicians would most likely significantly pick up the beat and by then conversation would be difficult. No one yet was on the dance floor.

The waiters were beginning to approach the tables to fill wine and water glasses in preparation for the meal that would be served. The beat of the bodhrán drum was starting to irritate Jessica's nerves like the *drip-drip* of a leaky water tap as she sat at the table. The melody of the other instruments wasn't preventing her from waiting for every tap of the musician's hand on the drum. Every beat seemed to thump in her head as the musician hit the instrument again and again. Stanley and Frankie still weren't there. And Jessica was sorry that Stanley wasn't able to comment on the music that the quintet continued to play. Maybe if the pianist explained the background of the music to her, she wouldn't focus so much on the drum's incessant beating. But still the pair didn't enter the room.

Finally, Jessica felt like she couldn't sit still any longer, and she got up from her seat and leaned over to Dev and Amy. "I'm just going to go back to the hall and see what might be keeping Stanley and Frankie from joining us."

No sooner had the words left her lips than she turned around and saw Stanley suddenly burst into the dining room. Even from her distance from him, Jessica could see that he was sweating profusely and his hair was matted to his forehead. His plaid bow tie was now askew, as though he had been pulling at it to allow him to breathe without any constriction. He seemed to take a long, deep breath and then yelled out loud and clear for everyone in the dining room to hear, "*Help! Help! I've found Frankie. I don't think she's breathing!*"

Eleven
Flashback to the Past

essica was in Frankie's bedchamber. She was not alone; Stanley was there. The man was totally distraught and seemed unable to comprehend that the symphony of events swirling around him bore more elements of cacophony than any gentle melody he might compose in romantic moments. Dev Matthews, ever the dedicated physician of his community, was attempting to take charge of the bizarre situation. Also, there were the Ryans and Amy Stanwich huddled in one area of the room. Jessica and Matthews were able to learn that Lora had obtained a pass key to open Frankie's door at Stanley's agitated insistence when Frankie hadn't materialized. And the two had been the first to find the writer. Lora was practically shaking in her shoes. It was clear the young girl was unable to believe what she and Stanley had come upon so unexpectedly; it was nothing she had yet experienced in her life.

Frankie was sprawled on the floor of the room. Dev and Jessica, who had both led the charge up to the woman's bedchamber after Stanley's frantic cry for help, had confirmed Frankie to be pulseless and breathless. They had been unable to resuscitate the writer despite their most valiant efforts. Matthews had called the local police station and the police were now on their way to Castle Ryan to assess the situation for themselves.

"This has never happened before," Brenda wailed, her hands clasping each other so tightly that her knuckles appeared white in the dimly lit room. "The poor woman. The poor woman," she kept repeating to herself. "I still can't believe this happened."

"Keep calm, Brenda," her husband, Bevin, admonished. "The police should be here any minute now. They'll figure everything out. They'll figure it all out." He had inadvertently picked up his wife's repetitive litany.

Their son and daughter were standing as close as possible to their parents. The two young people were frozen in place. Alice looked shell-shocked as she nervously clutched her mother's arm. Joel looked like he was finally getting to see what he had only imagined by reading all of his crime thrillers, and the result wasn't as thrilling as he had expected. To Jessica they both suddenly looked like children who were experiencing something beyond their understanding, and they needed to be as close as possible to the safety and security of their parents' presence.

"We should get the others out into the corridor," Dev said quietly to Jessica. He jerked his head authoritatively toward the open door to the corridor. "The local police should be arriving shortly as Bevin said. The fewer people in this room until they arrive, the better."

"Yes. You're right. Of course. Let me help you."

Jessica and Dev began to herd the others out of the room and into the hallway. Amy was the last to leave Frankie's bedchamber. She was standing with her back to all the others. The folds of her lavender crêpe gown were motionless about her bulky frame. She was leaning over slightly to get a better look at Frankie. Jessica moved back over to Amy to encourage the older woman to join the others exiting the room. But Amy wasn't budging an inch. The eyes in her large head were fixated on the motionless body lying on the floor in such disarray.

"Look at her," Amy said. "Look at her!" Her hand was pointed toward Frankie's inert form so that the black stones of the rings on Amy's fingers shone like the hard shells of beetles in the still dim light of the room. "Why, look at what she's wearing!"

All heads now turned back toward the body. Frankie was dressed in a long, cream-colored gown adorned with a buttercup-yellow sash about the waist and white lace at the collar. The dress was slightly longer than the length of Frankie's inert form and the hem dangled sadly over her outstretched feet that disappeared under the folds of fabric.

"What do you mean?" Jessica asked.

"Why, my dear, I guess you haven't seen the painting that hangs in the best antiques shop around here." Amy clucked her tongue. Suddenly her observation seemed to gain more importance to her than the still form lying on the floor of the bedchamber. "It's the dress Evelyn Lansing wore when she had her portrait painted. Although the one in the painting has more of a mauve shade to it than this one does." She again pointed her finger in the direction of the body. "But otherwise, that dress is exactly like the one in the portrait. The painting's in the shop for all to see. Paul Callahan—the man who runs the shop—keeps it there as a tourist draw. I've seen it many times myself whenever I've popped into his shop. He's always trying to cajole me into selling him some of my small treasures, you see. But he's a gentleman, so now and then, he wins me over."

Jessica looked back at the body lying on the floor. Frankie's hair had been styled in an elaborate arrangement of curls, with a chignon on the top, toward the back of her head, all of which had been horribly disarranged by the attempts to resuscitate her. But there was no mistaking that the original effect had been that of a Victorian lady's coiffure. *That was odd*, Jessica thought—and so unlike what she would have expected of the writer who had only seemed interested in what her pen put on paper.

Jessica knelt down to take a better look at the dress Frankie was still wearing. She was careful not to further disturb Frankie's body. The dress, in its styling, certainly looked as though it came from a much earlier time. But the fabric was new, without evidence of any discoloration of age. Jessica was certain of that.

Jessica got up from the floor. And as she looked up, her gaze landed on a drinking glass that she hadn't first noticed in the other part of the room. It was sitting on the edge of the vanity table by the window in the corner. The vanity was similar to the one in Jessica's bedchamber. It was a delicate piece of furniture with a clear-glass top and a gathered fabric skirt. The fabric was pale in color so that the drinking glass on the table, made of brilliant, greenish crystal, stood out in contrast. The glass was also similar to one in Jessica's room. She walked over to better examine it. As she peered inside the depths of the glass, Jessica saw a smear of white, milky liquid clinging to the bottom of the glass and around its lower sides.

"Dev," Jessica called out over her shoulder to get the attention of the other doctor in the room.

Matthews came over immediately and Jessica pointed down into the glass. He didn't say anything, but after also peering carefully inside, he nodded to her. It was clear their minds were on the same page. Then he said, "Let's clear this room *now*." He shooed the others away; they had slowly returned after hearing Amy's outburst. "Lora, the room needs to be locked." Turning to the Ryans, who were still huddled together as a group, he added firmly, "No one is to come inside this room until the police arrive. *And I mean no exceptions.*"

****

Detectives Byrne and Smith of the Gardá Síochána, the civilian police force of the Republic of Ireland, diligently made their inspection of Frankie's bedchamber. The two men, both with brown hair and blue eyes and of a similar height and age so that it was difficult to tell one from the other except by their names, showed minimal emotion as they surveyed the room and Frankie's body. The body was still lying in the center of the room where it had first been discovered. The noise from the creaking of the floorboards, as the two detectives' generous frames moved about the room from its edges to its center, was compensated for by the lack of any other sounds in the room. There was only the occasional brief remark they exchanged with each other.

They called in their medical and investigative personnel, who carefully removed the body and what evidence they needed. And before leaving the estate, the two detectives promised the Ryans to be in touch with them with any pertinent information as it became available.

The guests, who had come for an evening of dinner and dancing, were still in various states of shock. What had begun as a promised night of enchantment had devolved into absolute chaos and disbelief. Those who lived locally provided contact information and then quickly decamped for their homes; they were obviously eager to review the events of the night in private and deprived themselves of the ghoulish pleasure of lingering to obtain the additional details they might glean by remaining on the premises.

Those staying at the castle and Amy Stanwich—who must have considered her adjacent cottage as linked to the estate and thus part of the more intimate coterie involved with the sad event of the evening—settled into the small library off the main hall. It was a room that Jessica hadn't been in before. It was unexpected that so peaceful and contemplative a room as the library appeared, with its large fireplace and massive bookshelves lining the walls, was now put to use for those left to recover from the shock that they had received that night.

The Ryans insisted on providing copious quantities of brandy in an attempt to regain a trace of normalcy or, perhaps, just sedation of the senses. So in front of the large stone fireplace that was balanced on either side by the shelves of books, the group consisting of Jessica, Dev Matthews, Amy Stanwich, Stanley Bogart, all four Ryans, Louis Aspen, and Michael Thornes sat on upholstered chairs and sofas in the room. They were huddled around a coffee table on which the large decanter of brandy sat, so far untouched. The amber liquid in the crystal decanter sparkled. It reflected the light rays that hit it from the chimney fire that flickered off the wood in the fireplace. The fire occasionally let off a spark or two. Its warmth was comforting to the guests, despite that even with the late hour the temperature outside remained gentle and very little cold crept into the room.

Jessica scanned the faces about her that were staring absently into the ether. Only missing were those of the gardener, Alvin Hill, who had not presented himself, and Lora, who had returned to the kitchen to salvage what she could of the food that would not be needed that night.

"This is unbelievable," Brenda said. "I still can't get my head around what happened tonight. I know I keep repeating myself, but it's true. We've never had a death in the castle ever since we've run it as an inn and certainly never one like this, have we, Bevin?" She looked at her husband for emotional support, but he remained silent. She continued to rub her right knee back and forth with her hand in agitation. It was as though the earlier bravado she had displayed by wearing her high, stacked heels had now vanished with the reality of what had occurred at the castle. She seemed to totally crumble. And it was clear to anyone watching her that her bad knee was now more bothersome than ever, as though all her misery had transferred to the weakened joint.

Her husband removed his wife's hand from her knee and placed it within his own.

"Now Brenda, the castle *has* had its skeletons, hasn't it?" Amy said before Bevin could reply to his wife. She was not giving him the chance to finally do so.

"You're referring to Evelyn Lansing?" Louis asked.

"Why, of course I am. You can't have failed to notice how Frankie was dressed tonight. Why, anyone could see it for themselves. Well, look at me, and look at Jessica, and at Brenda and Alice. You don't see any of us outfitted in period costume, do you? No one expected this to be a costume ball, now did they? Frankie was clearly attired in the exact gown that Evelyn Lansing wore for her portrait that's in Callahan's antiques shop. I've already said that. But I guess just because I'm an old woman I have to repeat myself to be heard! *It's intolerable!* That's what it is."

"Now Amy, don't get so upset," Bevin said at last. "No one's ignoring what you're saying. We're all listening to you."

"Well, I should hope so!"

Louis and Michael said nothing. Stanley still appeared to be in shock. The pianist was absentmindedly pulling at his bow tie with fingers of both hands, which would not be playing any

music that night—and perhaps not for some time from the look
of him.

"Amy, I think I should get you home," Dev Matthews said,
preventing any further conversation. As her physician, he had
clearly decided to take full command of his elderly patient. "I
think it is time for you to go home and take a sleeping pill. I
want you to get some sleep. I think that's the best thing to do
for the time being."

Amy looked as though she was on the brink of protest,
but then she pursed her lips and said, "All right, Dev. I agree.
Let's go."

Dev helped her lift her bulky frame from the chair, and he
escorted her out of the library as all the others watched them
depart.

"I think he's got the right idea," Jessica said. "I, for one,
intend to take his very sensible advice and go to bed myself.
I think we all could benefit by some good, long rest tonight.
Stanley, would you be so kind as to walk me to my door?"
Jessica thought he looked like he was going to fall out of his
chair and collapse onto the floor, and the best way for him to
get some sleep was if he helped her to her room to get her own.

Bevin Ryan then stood up, reassuming his role as the pro-
prietor of Castle Ryan, and said, "Yes. Let's all do the same.
Whatever happens next, none of us can do anything about it
until the morning—or at least until we hear from the police.
They've promised to contact me as soon as they know anything.
They seem like good men. I'm sure they will."

Louis and Michael remained in their chairs while the others
reached the door and were congregating, waiting for the two to
join them. But the two men just surveyed the others. Then they
said, as if in one voice, "We'll stay here for a while. We have a
lot to think about."

Twelve
A Picture Might
Tell a Story

Jessica roused herself early the next morning from a troubled sleep. The horrific episode of the evening before had prevented any respite throughout the long night. As she lay in bed, she regretted not drinking some of the brandy the Ryans provided in the library; it would have helped quiet her mind. Finally, exhaustion triumphed over the tumultuous thoughts running through her brain, and merely from overwhelming fatigue, she drifted into unconsciousness. But it was fleeting, and she awoke several times. Each time she peered at the clock by her bed, surprised to see how little time had passed since she last checked it. Now still unrefreshed, she decided a long shower might clear her foggy head and wash away any lingering unease.

She got out of bed and entered the bath; it was so quiet in the room. Whatever noise she made fumbling with the faucets to the tap were muffled by the thick tiles and wainscoting around the walls. She looked in the mirror that was hanging over the sink. She could see how haggard she looked without the refreshment of a good night's sleep; there was puffiness under her eyes. She poked around the cabinet behind the mirror to see if the castle might have some soothing lotion that might remove the puffiness, but she couldn't find any and slammed the cabinet door back into place in frustration. She picked up a small bar of fragrant soap that was nestled in a porcelain dish. It had a calming lavender scent and might help to wash away the fuzziness she still felt.

Suddenly, as she looked again in the mirror, she no longer saw her own face. *It was Frankie Alexis's pale face staring back at her.* The writer's countenance was frozen by the mask of death in a horrible expression of anguished pain; it was a worse vision than any she had seen the night before on the dead woman's face.

Jessica jumped back in fright, hitting the back of her shins against the sides of the bathtub and almost falling backward into it. She managed to right herself by gripping madly at the heated towel rack that was bolted to the floor. Little did she know when she had admired it that it was to be the means of preventing her from breaking her neck. She shook her head back and forth, squeezing into the lids of her eyes with two knuckles of each of her forefingers until her vision cleared and she once again saw herself reflected in the mirror. She looked even worse than she had before. But at least it was her face that she saw and not that of a dead woman.

But Jessica couldn't easily remove from her brain the other images she remembered. She recalled the garb Frankie had worn. The dress hanging limply over Frankie's recumbent form was as clearly fixed in her brain as if she were looking at it in a book or magazine. She also remembered Amy noting that the dress resembled Evelyn Lansing's attire, which had been sealed into perpetuity by the painting of the woman now hanging in an antiques shop.

Evelyn Lansing's story was becoming too oft repeated to ignore. It seemed to have a strong connection to more than a few of the town's colorful inhabitants that she had met so far. Amy had mentioned that Evelyn's portrait was available for viewing. Jessica couldn't guess how it ended up in the antiques shop after all those years. Was it donated or sold to the store before or after the woman's death? Was it even still there? Maybe it had been sold since Amy had last seen it? Maybe Amy was mistaken that it was ever there? Whatever the history behind the portrait, Jessica knew, if Amy was correct and the portrait was still there and ready to be seen, she had to take a look at it for herself—and now.

Jessica quickly showered, forgetting the long one she had promised herself, and dressed, eager to see her plan through to completion now that she had fastened onto it. To get to the shop, she would once again have to approach Alvin Hill for the castle's car. That thought gave her only a moment's hesitation. "Don't be such a wimp, Jessica!" she scolded herself. She couldn't let the gruffness of his manner deter her. She was tougher than that. Also, she was starting to get her bearings around the town and its surrounding environs and was less afraid of getting lost on the roads than she had been.

Jessica pulled out her cell phone, searched the internet, and found the directions to Callahan's antiques shop; she could easily make it there. The shop was called the Gold Harp, and just as Amy had said, it was owned by a man named Paul Callahan. As luck would have it, the shop was open early that morning. Jessica tossed the cell phone into her purse, grabbed her room key, and left her room after taking one last look around it. A cold shudder ran through her as she realized how similar her room looked to the one Frankie had inhabited until so recently.

Jessica wondered for a moment if she should knock on Stanley's door to see how he was doing. He had looked so distraught the night before. And she could guess the pianist had passed an even more troubled sleep than she had. His association with the writer had obviously been greater, although by how much Jessica couldn't know. But she held back, deciding that the best thing to do was to give the man some space to grieve in private. So she quietly passed his door and headed down the stairs to the main hall to see who else was about.

Alice Ryan was manning the reception desk that morning, and luckily Brenda's daughter still had the car keys that Jessica had previously returned. Neither spoke much except to pass the ignition key from one to the other. It was clear the sad event of the previous night had taken its toll on congenial conversation. Alice looked in no mood to linger and pass the time of day with any guest. The girl's usual friendliness was replaced by an aura of muted efficiency. Still with the car keys in hand, Jessica was relieved to think she would only have to get the car itself from Alvin Hill's domain. She preferred the young girl's silence to the gardener's probable impatience at being interrupted again from his work just to hunt up keys to the castle's loaner car.

Jessica left the castle. She quickly walked back around it to the shed. But she was soon disappointed to see that Hill was there, even at this early hour. He was just finishing cleaning up from washing the car Jessica now wanted to borrow.

"Hello, Mr. Hill," Jessica said to him as politely as she could muster, hoping to ingratiate herself with the man.

As she expected, he was brusque in his reply. "No need for 'Mr. Hill.' Alvin's good enough for me. We've met before. Did you think I'd forget you so soon? I haven't lost my marbles yet, you know."

"No. I didn't think that. Not at all. It's only that Alice lent me the car keys to use the car again. Are you finished with it? I don't want to trouble you, but I'd like to take it to town again. I have an errand to run." She realized she was rambling a bit.

But somehow, in his presence, she couldn't stop herself. *Maybe she wasn't as tough as she liked to think?*

"I just washed it. But I guess a car's meant for driving, so it should be used when it's needed. I don't want it out looking dirty though. That wouldn't reflect good on me. People around here will think I'm not doing my job. I wouldn't like that. People around here talk a lot, you know. It's a small town. Not like Dublin."

"Oh. I don't think anyone would think that, Alvin."

"Well. You never know about people, now do you? They can surprise you."

"No. I guess you don't."

He walked away and Jessica opened the door and got into the car. As she put the key in the ignition and the engine revved into gear, she thought, *Now why did he say that?*

****

Once again, Jessica followed GPS directions into town as transmitted from her cell phone's audio speaker. She was becoming accustomed to the strangely pronounced, staccato landmarks that were barked out to her from the phone. They served as goalposts leading her on, and as she passed each one, confidence in her sense of direction increased exponentially. She drove past Millie's coffee shop and passed a few other stores before turning off the engine in front of a storefront with a large, glass window to the left of the entrance door. Above the window was a bright-blue, wooden frame upon which were carefully emblazoned gold letters in Gothic font that assured her she had reached the Gold Harp.

The antiques shop looked like any she might have seen in small towns in the United States. It had the same slightly rough-about-the-edges appearance. There was an odd mix of clutter visible through the glass window: an upholstered chair, a case of bric-a-brac with its heavy weight tottering on skinny legs, bits of jewelry, glassware, and silverware, all in carefully staged disarray. The soft lighting in the shop was strong enough so there was no ignoring the patina of age encrusted on the many display items.

Jessica looked farther inside the shop and saw the clutter continued with a narrow aisle that led away from the window; it was in between more objects on either side but seemed to allow navigation from front to back. She could just make out the opening to a small room at the very end. And she wondered if that was where the most prized items were kept away from prying street eyes, and if Evelyn Lansing's portrait that she was so eager to see might be hanging there. As hard as she tried, she couldn't see anything that might be the painting on either of the two long walls within her view. So she figured it was time to go inside and find it with Paul Callahan's assistance.

Jessica pulled open the door and entered the shop. It was even darker inside once the heavy door shut tightly behind her. The sunlight that shone through the display window seemed to be sucked up like a vacuum cleaner by all the items around her. She needed to wait a while for her eyes to adjust to the dimness, and she blinked several times until she was finally acclimated to the cluttered surroundings. The narrow passage between the various antiques allowed her to move hesitantly toward the back of the shop. The last thing she wanted to do was to knock over anything onto the floor. She had no clue as to how valuable each piece was. But she couldn't imagine it would be easy to ingratiate herself with Callahan if her first introduction to the man was for an estimation of inventory damage.

As she carefully moved along, she still didn't see a painting that might be of Evelyn Lansing. At the very end of the aisle was the small room she thought she had spied from outside.

As she looked up from covering her path toward it, she noticed a diminutive man now stood in front of the room. His appearance made Jessica think of a tiny gnome inhabiting the interior of the earth and guarding its precious treasures; she guessed he must be Paul Callahan.

He flashed her a welcoming smile that she took as an encouraging sign that she hadn't caused any unnoticed damage. Tight curly hair extended from the top of his head to either side of his face in an almost perfect circle like a little clay planter growing miniature circular shrubbery around its borders. His face had many lines and furrows running across it, as though the age of the items in the shop was reflected in every crease of his visage. It struck her that she could almost take a marker and draw lines along them with perfect precision. But somehow the effect wasn't unpleasant because the wrinkles suggested sagacity rather than age.

"May I help you?" he asked.

"Yes. Yes, you may. Would you be Paul Callahan, the owner of the store?"

"Yes, himself."

"Fabulous. I heard about your antiques shop, the Gold Harp."

"Wonderful. Evidently, this is it. From whom did I receive the recommendation that led you here?"

"From Amy Stanwich."

"Ah, *Amy*. Now she's quite a character, that one. Isn't she? But I like her."

"Yes, she is. She mentioned that you had a portrait of Evelyn Lansing in your shop. I was interested in taking a look at it, if I might."

"I gather you've been informed about our local history. You do *know* it's not for sale, don't you? I wouldn't want to give you the wrong impression."

"Oh, I'm not wanting to purchase it. That's not why I'm here. But I have heard about it. You see, I'm staying at Castle Ryan. And so obviously I was curious about it, and I hoped you'd let me take a look. If it isn't too much trouble that is."

"Of course. It isn't any trouble at all. I would be only too happy to show it to you. To be honest, it is *quite* a draw to my shop. And that's why I'll never sell it. Never. Come back here into this room. The painting is hanging by my desk. I like to look at it myself. That's why I keep it in here. It makes my day just to fix my eyes on it now and then."

He moved away from the opening in the inner doorway to allow Jessica to pass by him. As soon as she entered the small room, she couldn't miss it. The portrait was hanging in a point of prominence on an otherwise blank wall to her left. There were no other paintings in the room to compete with it. But even if there were, Jessica knew at one glance they wouldn't be able to, no matter how hard they tried. The wall Evelyn's portrait was hung on was painted a pale gray so that it almost seemed that the pallor of a cloudy day was serving as backdrop for the intricately carved, gilded frame encasing the painting. And the effect was almost that of a golden doorway beckoning one into another world.

The portrait of Evelyn Lansing was painted in full length. It was a brave rendering of a young woman who, though not truly beautiful, had *a presence*. The portrait commanded to be examined more closely; it seemed to be owed that. Evelyn's dark hair was piled high above her head, just as Frankie's had been arranged the night of the party. Jessica felt a frisson of cold run down the back of her neck, despite the closeness of the small, windowless room at the back of the shop. And as Amy had correctly described, Evelyn's mauve dress looked almost the same as the one Frankie had worn when her dead form was discovered. There was the same bright-yellow sash around the tiny waist and white lace collar around the long neck of the woman in the portrait. But the mauve color of the dress in Evelyn's portrait was so much deeper, making Jessica envision endless fields of lavender. She could almost smell the sweetly perfumed scent floating through the air of the little back room.

Evelyn Lansing was half turned to the viewer as she leaned over a battlement. She was looking down at the landscape below. It appeared almost as if she were a soldier watching for a battalion of advancing troops to dare to enter her domain. Jessica tried but failed to remember if Castle Ryan's roof had any features similar to what was depicted in the portrait. Might Evelyn have posed for the portrait on the very top of the castle? Or did the scene owe itself to the artist's imagination, which had been deployed to create his subject's dramatic tableau?

"It's quite a masterpiece, isn't it?" Callahan asked quietly, interrupting Jessica's study of the painting and bringing her back to the present with a slight shock. *How long had she been mesmerized by it?* She couldn't fathom a guess.

"Yes. It is," Jessica finally said. "May I ask what you know about the painting's provenance?"

"Of course. It was painted by a rising young artist who clearly was enamored of his subject. You can see that from the way he posed her, even if I hadn't told you that. She looks like a queen, doesn't she? In fact, he titled it *Queen Evelyn*. Yes, I believe that's what he wrote on the back of the canvas. His signature is on the lower right side of the painting. But his name doesn't really matter. He never attained great fame on his own as an artist. It was his subject that brought out his greatness. His other works weren't much to speak of. Also sad, isn't it?"

He didn't wait for an answer but began speaking in a rapid but clear diction. "Getting back to Evelyn, she was quite an unusual woman for her time. That much is known. Evelyn wrote stories that she would read to her guests as entertainment.

Supposedly there was quite a lot of entertainment at the castle in her day. Not much else to do at that time, I guess, without television and the internet. So person-to-person interaction in large social settings was more a part of life than it is now. Also, sad. Anyway, the story goes that Evelyn decided she wanted to publish what she had written—and under her own name. Heavens!" He threw up his hands in mock dismay. "Apparently, there was a publisher who was a fan of her writing, and of *her* as well. Come to think of it, I wonder if he also had a competition going with the portrait painter. Who knows about that? She was apparently discrete enough—if there was anything there—that there was no scandal, or if there was, I could never find out anything about it. Anyway, unfortunately she ended up dead before any of her writings were published. So that's all I can tell you about her."

"Yes. I've heard about her death. But how exactly did she die? Is that known? Did she sicken and die of natural causes, or was she strangled, drowned, or even pushed off some parapet? Like this one." Jessica pointed to the painting.

"My dear, you are a blunt person, now aren't you? But in answer to your question, no. She was discovered on the grounds behind the castle. I do know that. She had apparently succumbed to the elements. There was a storm the night she died. But what was she doing outside alone like that in the first place? Now *that is the question*, as the bard said. Was she meeting someone clandestinely? Maybe one or the other of the two I mentioned? Had she been led out there on some nefarious ruse? Did she want to end her life? It was never clear, and no one was ever charged with murder. But the locals always had, and still have, their doubts about the details of what happened that night."

"And how did you come to get the portrait in your shop?"

"Oh, that I *can* answer for you. After Evelyn was dead, her husband, Bailey—that was his name—sold the castle. Then it passed through a variety of different hands until the Ryans finally obtained it and turned it into an inn for guests like yourself. My father was always on the lookout for items that had been there in Evelyn's time. And he serendipitously came upon the portrait. I'm not really sure exactly how. But he told me never to sell it. And it was very good advice that he gave me. I've always followed it. As I said, it's a good draw for tourists like yourself. It does tend to bring them into the shop. That's another reason why I have it in the back of the store. You have to pass through the entire length of the store to see it." He chuckled with obvious satisfaction at his mercantile skill. "Now are you interested in anything else?"

"Oh yes. Oh yes." Jessica shook her head up and down.

"Good!"

"I guess it's only fair that after I've taken up so much of your time to assuage my curiosity, I owe it to you. What do you suggest I look at?"

"Let me think." He placed his right forefinger to his thin, pursed lips to accentuate his deep thought process. "I know. I have just the thing. Come with me."

Callahan led her back to the front of the store and to the display window that Jessica had first peered through from the other side. He leaned into it and reached into the corner for one of the small pieces of jewelry that were carefully arranged on a bright-green velvet cloth on which no dust had been allowed to accumulate. He gently picked up a delicate, black-beaded bracelet and handed it to Jessica's waiting palm.

"Women usually like bracelets, don't they, so that they can wear them all the time? It's Victorian, you know. Lovely, isn't it? And not too dear in cost as well. I think you'll not find anything finer for twice the price at any of those fancy shops in Dublin! I pride myself on the value I give my customers. That's why my shop is still here after all these years. I don't play any games!"

Jessica turned the bracelet around in her hand. It was a delicate piece of jewelry. It had a small, gold clasp of the older type that hooked around the other side of the locking mechanism and then snapped into place to securely encircle the wrist without fear of being lost. The beads were jet-black like the midnight sky. But the light that managed to shine through the window caught them so that they sparkled brilliantly in her hand as she turned the bracelet over and over. Jessica looked up from the bracelet and back to Callahan, who was smiling broadly; he was displaying the satisfaction of the weathered shopkeeper who could read his clientele with the expertise of many years of hawking his wares.

"Yes," Jessica said. "This speaks to me. I think I'll take it."

Thirteen
The Police Return

Jessica drove back to Castle Ryan, where she saw an empty police car parked on the gravel drive in front. She pulled her car in next to it and hurried into the castle just as detectives Smith and Byrne were leaving. Both policemen studiously ignored the questioning look she threw their way as they squeezed past her. So she had no other option but to approach Brenda and Bevin, who were together at the reception desk. She was eager to learn any information the two detectives might have left with the castle's proprietors; she didn't want to miss a single detail.

"Good afternoon," Jessica said. "I'm returning the car keys. I left the car just outside."

"Oh. Thank you. I'll let Alvin know to pick up the keys and the car if you're finished with it." Brenda's body wasn't following the direction of her words because, after several unsuccessful attempts at placing the keys back in their container, her husband finally took them from her shaking hands and dropped them back into the box himself.

"I see the detectives were here," Jessica said, looking back over her shoulder to where the policemen had recently exited.

"Yes," Bevin said, almost curtly.

But his wife was much more interested in relaying the information the policemen had delivered. Brenda looked around her as though she still wanted to keep what she had learned within the thick walls of the castle. Then she whispered with a conspiratorial look on her face, so that her mobile lips seemed to do more of the talking than her own voice box, "They found residue of *sleeping pills* in that glass that was left on her vanity table. The cause of death was an *overdose!* Can you believe that? I can't!"

"Now Brenda," her husband admonished. "In the first place, you probably shouldn't be talking, and in the second, try not to be so dramatic."

"Well, how else would you like me to be, Bevin? And I can say what I want, can't I? They didn't say it was a state secret, now did they?"

Jessica remained silent. She was mulling over Brenda's words. Then she said quietly, "That's funny, don't you think? I mean the glass being there like that certainly suggests she *might* have ingested something. But somehow, she just didn't seem to me like the type to take sleeping pills—and certainly not to overdose."

"No, she didn't!" Brenda said, shaking her head back and forth vigorously and totally ignoring her husband's exasperated look. "I agree with you entirely!"

"Now Brenda," her husband repeated. "You know what they told us. The door was locked from the inside. She had to have taken them. No one else could have gotten into her room. You're getting to sound just like Joel. No doubt you've been reading one of his silly, old crime books—just like he spends too much time doing when he should be helping out more with all the work about this place and leaving most of it for the rest of us to do, I might add."

He turned to Jessica. "They said they didn't have anything to make them think there was any *foul play* whatsoever." He then turned back to his wife. "That's the term Joel would use, wouldn't he, Brenda? And besides, Lora said Frankie didn't ask to have anything brought to her to drink. So at the very least, we know nothing came from our kitchens. That's the main thing that I'm thinking about at this point. At least, we can thank our lucky stars for that!"

"Oh really, Bevin? That's what you're most concerned about? Not about the fact that a woman is dead? And if you're going to be just thinking about Castle Ryan's reputation, *how do you think we'll get people to stay at your precious castle if they end up dead staying here?*"

"Now you know I didn't mean it like that," Bevin said.

But Brenda didn't give him a chance to apologize. Instead, she snapped down the upper part of the counter, which had been up on its hinges. And she left her husband, managing to walk away more quickly than Jessica had ever seen before, despite the woman's poor right knee.

Jessica found herself alone with Bevin. He looked at her as though totally bemused by the parting image of his wife rapidly thumping away from him in anger. Jessica guessed it was an uncommon occurrence. Frankie's demise was clearly taking its toll on the unity of the family Ryan's close-knit circle. The eldest Ryan seemed seriously embarrassed at having Jessica witness an argument between husband and wife.

"I'm sorry for that," he finally said. "Sometimes the stress and strain of running this place gets the better of all of us. The last thing we needed was this unfortunate thing to happen—just when it looked like we were finally getting the place to start paying off for itself. It's a true pity. And I do care what happened to that poor woman despite what the wife just said."

"I know you do," Jessica said.

Bevin then surveyed the large entrance hall around him, as though the likely financial burdens within its walls were a weight on his shoulders almost too heavy to bear. "Anyway, thank you very much for returning the keys to me." As an afterthought, he continued, "By the way, Mr. Aspen and Mr. Thornes were looking for you earlier. They should still be sitting in the library. You'll probably find them there even now."

"Thank you. I'll go look for them." She left Bevin and was suddenly painfully aware that she hadn't given any recent thought to the two men's proposal that they had presented to her, and to which they were most likely eagerly awaiting her response. It was time to get off the proverbial fence.

****

Jessica entered the library. How very different the room looked now from what it had on that fateful other night. Then the light had been so much dimmer, almost unnatural, with the light from the lamps reflecting off the anxious faces of those who had gathered there after Frankie's body had been discovered in her bedchamber. Now the library was not artificially illuminated. Instead, the full, bright light of day streamed through the large windows on either side of the fireplace and bookshelves. There was no longer an air of despondency in the otherwise warm room. The furniture was arranged just as it had been the night before when the guests and staff congregated over brandy, in shock from the events that had occurred. But in the light of day, and no longer a place for emotional recovery, the room seemed innocuous enough to Jessica's senses.

Louis and Michael were seated in neighboring club chairs,

deep in discussion, but both men looked up at her as Jessica came into the room.

"So here you are, Jessica," Louis said. He was once again the producer taking charge of any situation that needed his attention. He was clearly telegraphing that, although he and Michael were a team, it was he who was the decision-maker of the two men. "Please sit down. So have you come to a decision about the project we presented to you? Or are there any questions you might have that we still need to address? We can do that now. It's time, I think."

She sat down on the sofa directly across from them. The three heads were almost on the same level, and Jessica took comfort in that. She was surprised that she was able to notice that small detail in light of the last conversations that had occurred in that room. It was as though her natural instincts, which had propelled her through many an interview, both as interviewer and interviewee, had been ready just below the surface and able to pop up at a moment's notice when necessary.

Michael was looking at her as expectantly as Louis was, even though, so far, it was only Louis who was doing the talking. It was clear to her that they were both, at the very least, emotionally invested in the project. "Yes," Jessica said. "I have come to a decision. I want to let you both know that I am willing to proceed with the project."

"Great!" Both men gave her encouraging smiles. And Louis even hazarded a confident thumbs-up.

Jessica knew she had to immediately interject her caveat before Louis was able to lapse into any further florid details. So she said, "*But,*" putting extreme emphasis on the word, "I think it would be a good idea to bring Alain Raynaud in—as you suggested, but *now.*" Again, the emphasis. "I would feel uncomfortable giving you a total green light without him being here to do so at the same time."

"Totally understandable. Totally understandable," Louis repeated, confidence in his success emanating from his lips. "How soon can he get here to meet with us?"

"If you are both OK with a short delay, I'm going to call him immediately after we finish here and see if I can get him to come down for the weekend. Would that work for you both? I don't see how I can get him here any sooner than that."

"I think it would work. Don't we agree, Michael?" Louis looked at his partner, who gave his concurrence by a firm up-and-down nod.

"Fine. That's settled," Jessica said. "So why don't I go call Alain now and ask him to join us as soon as he can?" She got up from her chair to indicate she was on the job.

"Perfect. Perfect. You do so. We'll be on tenterhooks until he arrives at the castle."

****

Now that Jessica had arranged for Alain to join her, she realized how alone she had been feeling up to that point. Suddenly, the knowledge that Alain would soon arrive took a large burden off her shoulders, and she felt as though she could easily swim the English Channel.

"Now that's an idea!" she said to herself, remembering Brenda Ryan's suggestion to try out the spa's swimming pool when Jessica had first arrived at the castle.

Jessica picked up the phone in her room and called down to the reception desk. She found Brenda on duty and from her voice, Brenda had cooled off since she had last sparred with her husband.

"Brenda, I decided I do want to take a swim in the indoor pool. But I didn't bring a swimsuit and you had mentioned that Alice keeps some on hand for guests to purchase."

"Yes, she does. You look like you're a size eight. Am I right?"

"Exactly on the mark."

"Good. I'll have Alice leave a few choices down by the spa. Just pick the one you like and leave the tag on the desk. And we'll add it to the room charge. If Mr. Aspen has a problem, we can sort it out later. Just so you know though, with all that's happened we're still at sixes and sevens, so there's no one on duty down there. So just be safe swimming by yourself."

"Don't worry. I'm a good swimmer."

"That's a relief. I couldn't take another tragedy. Then have fun."

Jessica put down the phone, left the room, and took the elevator down to the lower level. As Brenda had said, the spa was deserted. True to the woman's word, three bathing suits were neatly arranged on the counter. Alice had obviously been quick on her toes. Jessica chose a simple black maillot that looked like it would fit, snapped off the tag, and left it on the counter. Then she grabbed a clean towel and made for the pool.

She pushed through the swinging door to the changing room and went inside. The room was paneled in cedar wood with a long bench in the middle. Jessica quickly changed into the swimsuit, left her clothes in one of the lockers, and pushed through another door to find a pool that must have been at least fifty feet in length but only about fifteen feet across.

The pool was a pretty affair with aquamarine tiling around the perimeter. But what was most striking were the murals on the walls on either side of the pool. Rather than a standard white, the walls were painted with scenes of nature, so that it almost seemed as though she would be swimming among the castle's outdoor gardens rather than in the lower level of the building.

Now I won't dive, she thought, remembering Brenda's admonishment to play it safe. "Better not hit my head, or she'll never forgive me," Jessica chuckled to herself. *When did I develop such bad taste?* she thought, shaking her head at her own ghoulish humor.

Jessica walked carefully around the edge of the pool to the deeper end and emersed herself in the water. She proceeded to swim back and forth across the length of the pool. The water was warm but not hot, and it felt refreshing as she swam each lap. Raising each arm over her head, she continued swimming back and forth, her head rising and falling back into the water. With each rise of her head, she caught a glimpse of the painted natural scenes on the walls that seemed to bring her out of herself.

Finally, out of breath, she stopped swimming and emerged her head again from the water. She clutched at the side of the pool and breathed in great quantities of the humid, indoor air around her. She had failed to complete the last lap. She was spent. Pushing her wet hair back from her face and wiping the drops of pool water from her eyes, she blinked several times to bring her vision back into focus. Suddenly she swore that she could make out a dark shadow flittering across the wall across from her and moving between the different painted details of the mural.

Jessica jerked her body quickly around in the pool and forced her vision to totally clear. She didn't see anyone. *Had she seen anything before? Had anyone come into the pool area? Was she no longer alone, even now?* She didn't hear anything and she hadn't heard anything before. She was sure of that. But she had been under water for so much of the time. And all she could now see across from her was the same painted murals on either side of the pool room as she looked back and forth. They were just simple scenes of nature. She saw nothing to be afraid of, and certainly no one else was there now. She was still totally alone. She blinked again and breathed deeply in and out to restore the calm that she had so quickly lost.

Had there been a shadow? If so, of what? Had it been of a woman? A man? An animal? She couldn't be certain any longer of what she might have seen. All she knew was that she had better get out of the pool—and now! She swam over to the shallow end of the pool and jumped out.

Dripping with the water that no longer felt so refreshing, but only chilled her, she grabbed the towel that she had left on one of the deckchairs by the water's edge. She hugged the large, white towel around her. Its cottony thickness was soft and comforting, but she was still determined to get away from the pool room as quickly as she could.

Whatever she did next, she determined, she would never again put herself in such a situation until Alain had joined her and she was no longer alone.

Fourteen
Raynaud Joins In

"**A**lain," Jessica called out. As she stood on the front steps of Castle Ryan and waved her right hand back and forth over her head, she realized how happy she was to see him finally arrive.

Inspector Alain Raynaud closed the door to the taxi that had just deposited him at the castle. Raynaud looked back at Jessica and smiled broadly. He was holding a leather carry-on small enough so that she realized with some disappointment that he would probably not stay much longer than the weekend.

The taxi took off, heading back to Dalkey and spraying up a small gust of gravel from the drive in its wake. Jessica went over to Alain and received a kiss and an embrace. Then she laughed and, pointing at the departing vehicle, said, "You in a taxi!"

"That's right."

"Well, that's a new sight for me. I'll have to put it in the record book to hold onto the documentation for the years to come."

"You told me that you borrowed a car here a couple of times."

"I did."

"So I figured you could be the driver should the need arise, which I'm sure it will. I have to admit that I'm still more comfortable on the right side of the road with the steering wheel on the left."

"Me too!"

He jerked his head toward the castle. "They have a room for me, or are we sharing?"

"Once you've met the Ryans for yourself, you'll understand why you're getting your own digs in this place. There's a quaint, old-fashioned quality to it."

"I would think so with what you've told me so far. *Especially* now that there's been a death on the estate!"

"That's not funny!" Jessica tried to kick him in his shins, but he avoided her low blow.

"But I'll agree it's been you who has sized up the situation."

"Thank you."

"So fair enough. You can make the rules—for the present."

"It's a deal."

"Anyway, now that I've flown all this way to get here, I hope you'll give me a few more details than those you shared over the phone about Aspen and Thornes and their ideas for us."

"Of course, I will."

"To be honest, I'm a little surprised that they're still contemplating the project at all, in light of what transpired."

"Oh, I don't think anything would make them give their plans up."

"Yes, but it smacks of bad taste. But of course, I'm no expert on the *sensibilities* of television producers."

"Oh. Don't worry about all that now. Let's go inside and get you checked in first. Then we can talk all about it."

They entered the castle, and Jessica watched Alain imme-diately size up the many elements of the main hall with his practiced, detective eye. As she did, she again noticed for herself the large staircase leading to the upper floor where many of the guest rooms were located, the broad reception desk, and the corridors leading off to the dining area and to the downstairs conference room and spa.

They went up to reception. True to expectations, Brenda, who was manning the desk, gave Alan a thorough once-over, seeming to notice his large frame, sandy-colored hair, and au-thoritative manner all in one glance. As pleasant as she was as she went through the motions of entering him as one of the castle's guests, there was no doubt that she expected he would be housed separately from Jessica. She placed him in a room in the opposite wing from Jessica; it was where the producer and the screenwriter had also been situated.

"I'll wait for you down here," Jessica said, receiving an ap-proving nod from Brenda.

"Fine."

"Once you're settled in, come back down." Jessica watched while Brenda led Alain to the elevator. His broad frame over-whelmed the smaller one in front of him as they entered the elevator and they disappeared behind its slowly closing doors.

A few minutes later, Alain returned without luggage. Jessica took his hand and led him back outside the castle and behind it. Then she said, "How about a walk? That way we can talk in private, and you can give your legs a good stretch from the plane ride."

"Fine with me. Sounds like a good idea."

"Excellent."

They began to trace the path which Jessica had taken the first day she arrived at the castle when she had followed the castle's brochure's neatly drawn diagrams that outlined the walking trails behind the estate. This time she was not alone, so she was more eager to hazard different routes than she had before. As they walked deeper and deeper into the wooded areas, they spied a squirrel scurrying about the bases of the trees. Its long, dark tail was splayed out behind its body as it dashed through the underbrush. And at one point, they caught sight of a small rabbit hurrying out of their way. At still another time, a rook flew over their heads and cawed, possibly warning some of his fellow birds in the trees of their approach.

Jessica now took Alain's arm and filled him in on what had been happening in his absence.

When she was done, Alain stopped, turned to face her, and said, "You didn't ask me to join you to discuss a television project about our prior *adventures*, did you?"

Jessica involuntarily looked down at her feet.

"You have a *new* one!"

She looked back up and took a deep breath because she knew her slight deception could go no further. "No, not really, I didn't ask you to come here *only* about the project. That's true."

"I knew it!"

"Well, I never thought you weren't sharp."

"Thank you. But don't you think the local police are fully capable of figuring out why your friend, Frankie, expired from an overdose of sleeping pills?"

"Well, no. I'm not so sure to tell you the truth."

"Why? Nothing you've shared with me so far suggests otherwise."

"I think it does."

"And I think you've gotten too used to handling matters as *you* think they should be handled rather than as those in authority do."

"That may be true. But there's more to it than meets the eye."

"Oh really?"

"Yes. I'm almost certain of that. The police are simply ignoring the way Frankie was dressed that night. Alain, it's as though they're unwilling to make any connection to Evelyn Lansing, which is *so obvious* to me. I told you about Amy Stanwich—she's the woman of advanced years who first mentioned that they were dressed so similarly—and then I saw the portrait of Evelyn Lansing. There was no mistaking it!"

"A connection to the writer who died here all those years ago?"

"Yes."

"What are you considering? *Ghost stories?* We are getting a little unnatural now, aren't we?"

"No, I don't think we are. Not exactly."

"Jessica—"

"I'll admit it sounds a little out of the ordinary. But you have to admit it smells funny: one writer staying at the castle dresses up in the very costume another writer wore in a famous—at least locally—portrait of her, who also died under suspicious circumstances, even if it was many years ago."

"Jessica—"

"Things are different around here, Alain. I told you that. I feel like there's a closer connection—and I know I'm repeating myself—to the past. Maybe it's because it's a small community. Or maybe it has something to do with Castle Ryan and its history. I just don't know."

Alain didn't say anything for a few minutes. He looked up above his head and studied the trees around them. A couple of robins, with their red breasts resembling shields against their brown feathers, flew from branch to branch over them. To Jessica, it was as though the birds were warbling tunes of encouragement. And she wondered if Alain was thinking the same because he finally said, "All right. I'll help you."

"Oh, Alain, thanks."

"Hold the gratitude for now. You know you can be very persuasive." He laughed. "I always do help, don't I? But we should start with Louis Aspen and Michael Thornes. I think that makes the most sense as a point of departure."

"OK."

"They're the two that brought you here—and now me, at least by extension of the fact. So they're the best ones to probe first. It's just too coincidental for them not to have some link— and I won't use the word *connection*—to what happened. You said it. I didn't. It 'smells funny.'"

"What will you say to them?"

"To begin with, I'll just meet them as they asked, and then we'll let *them* do the talking. Let's see if anything they say provides any clues to follow. That seems to me the most efficient way to go about this. Sounds all right to you?"

"All right with me."

"Good. So now let's get back to Castle Ryan and go find them. We've walked enough for now."

****

Jessica and Alain sat in the castle's library across from Louis Aspen and Michael Thornes. The two men were obviously pleased that she had been able to produce the inspector so quickly. Louis was practically smacking his lips as he spoke. Michael, though more reserved in his manner, was also watching for the new arrival's response to his partner's words. He was searching Alain's face almost as closely as his partner was himself.

"So Inspector Raynaud, I'm sure Jessica has filled you in on our idea for the television series we're contemplating," Louis said. Confidence was bubbling over in every syllable enunciated by the strong inflection of his voice.

"Yes, she has," Alain said. "And I'd like to say from the beginning that I'm skeptical about the project."

"*Skeptical?* I must admit I'm surprised by your use of that particular word. But you have kindly presented yourself here at our request. So we won't take it personally, will we, Michael?" Michael puckered his lips and shook his head left and right to indicate a *no*.

"Of course. Jessica asked me to come."

"And we are grateful to her for that."

"But both our private lives are just that—private."

"Oh. But the situations you have both been involved in recently could be the bases for such an exciting series. Just think about it! First, a murder on top of the majestic Mount Royal in Montreal, then a murder associated with a prestigious art fair in Miami, and most recently a murder at an elegant art museum in Paris! Those events practically write the screenplays themselves. Don't they, Michael?" He looked to his partner and once again received the required nod, quickly up and down, which seemed to be the expected mode of concurrence between the two men.

"And now one more death, eh?" Alain said.

"You are, of course, referring to the unfortunate loss of life of Frankie Alexis? That was so *tragic.*"

"To be sure."

"Well, from what I've learned from Bevin Ryan, the police are fairly certain that her death was self-induced. Locked room, sleeping pills, workaholic writer, etc., etc. What else can I say? But I grant you that it is a possible plot for an episode down the road. I'd be lying if I didn't admit that I am intrigued by that possibility."

Jessica tried to gauge if Louis's words were serious or not, but from his demeanor, she could only read true enthusiasm.

"But I guess time will tell how that plays out," Louis continued.

"Mr. Aspen—"

"Louis please!"

"Fair enough. I think the best thing for Jessica and me to do is for us to hold off for now as we seriously consider your proposal. Jessica has told me you both plan on remaining in the area for the near future, scouting out locations, etc. as she tells me your plots will be transposed to this location."

"Yes. That was a requirement of our largest financing partner."

"I see. Well, good. Give us some time for consideration of what you have presented to us, and we'll get you an answer as quickly as we can. And then we can go on from there. Jessica?"

"I totally agree."

"By the way, Louis, were you or Michael acquainted with Ms. Alexis previously before you arrived?"

"Why no," Louis said. "But Michael and I were aware of her work: crime stories and such. *Life copying fiction*, as they say. So ironic!"

Fifteen
Dublin's Fair City

ouis Aspen's production company was headquartered in Dublin. Jessica and Alain decided the next day that, as the city was fairly close to Dalkey, they would travel to the capital and scout out Aspen's offices. They journeyed north to Dublin via train after getting a lift from Alvin Hill in the castle's little, black car. Jessica gauged that Alain garnered more respect than she did from the gardener and that may have accounted for Alvin's improved attitude and the unexpectedly pleasant ride to the station.

As the train traversed the coastal landscape, Jessica and Alain discussed their plan.

"I think we should first concentrate on the areas surrounding Aspen's company," Jessica said. "Then we can *drop by* the offices to get a firsthand look at Aspen's holding."

"Makes sense. But you're sure you'll be able to keep your eyes focused on his company and not get distracted by all the other sights and sounds of the city?" He smiled at her.

She ignored his quip. "Of course, I'll be focused. But you're right. It's probably going to be a very different scene from Dalkey."

"Did Aspen give you any idea what his operation there is like when he first reached out to you?"

"No, not at all."

"There isn't much information about it that I was able to find. But at least, I didn't come upon any open or closed investigations. So that's a good sign."

"That is true."

The trip took about half an hour, and they were there almost before they knew it. Now they were standing in Dublin, on Grafton Street, from which it was a short step by foot to Aspen Productions.

Grafton Street was a major shopping drag. It was lined on either side of its full length with traditional, retro, and modern shops, many with a trendy flair. There were those selling thick, Irish sweaters with intricate cabled patterns, lace of all different varieties, and sturdy, tweed caps; others sold silver items, and still others hawked assortments of linen. Jewelry stores and flower stalls also dotted the pedestrian byway. They were clustered together, seemingly wherever there was a bit of free space.

On one corner a street musician was strumming his guitar to a jaunty Irish tune. He was doing it for the benefit of the passersby who occasionally stopped strolling the street to listen as he transitioned from tune to tune. Jessica pushed back in her mind any resemblance to the music that was played by the quintet of Irish musicians at Castle Ryan on the night that Frankie's body was discovered. This musician had his guitar case wide-open, and in it were a few spare euros hugging the crimson, velvet interior. The aficionados who had come to listen to him before Jessica dropped some coins inside the case. And Jessica followed suit by dropping in a few of her own. The musical jingle of coins as they hit the bottom of the case was reciprocated by an appreciative strum of the musician's guitar strings when his eyes mentally calculated the sum he received from the tourists.

"Come on," Alain said. "I thought you assured me you wouldn't get distracted."

"I'm not, but you're right."

He took her arm and they turned away from the guitar player.

Jessica and Alain headed up the street and wound their way over a few others, moving closer to the Liffey. The smell from the river wasn't unpleasant, despite its pungency. And the sun sparkled on the surface of the water, creating a linear line of shining light to guide them along the track of the river. They used the length of the waterway to keep their bearings as they walked along.

Finally, they came to the building they were looking for. It was a small, redbrick building. It faced the river, and it had a brass plaque to the side of the door advertising it as housing Aspen Productions. The door was painted a bright blue, and the bold color stood out from the rest of the building's rather nondescript Georgian façade. The color reminded her of the top of Paul Callahan's antiques shop, and she wondered for a moment if there had been a run on that particular lot of blue paint.

Jessica looked at the door to the building. Then she peered at Alain and asked, "What do you think? Shall we follow through and try to see if anyone's around today?"

"There's no time like the present. This was the plan. So let's do it."

"All right. So one more time, let's get our stories straight so we don't appear suspicious. We *decided* to see Dublin, and we were *walking* along the river, and we *realized* we were near the production company, and we *figured* we'd stop in and take a look at it. Right?"

"It's not great, but that's what we came up with and I think that it'll do."

She laughed. "That's not very encouraging. You don't like my plot narrative?"

"Enough. Just let me open the door."

"OK. OK. I only want to be prepared."

She went inside while he held the door open for her, and they found themselves in a small, poorly lit antechamber. It was a little disappointing considering the build-up Louis Aspen had already given them about himself back at Castle Ryan. There was a short panel of brass buzzers to the right of the inner glass door, each associated with individual businesses also headquartered in the building. Aspen Productions apparently only used one floor of the building's few office spaces and was located on the ground level. But its name was top on the list, and none of the other names under it rang a bell to Jessica or Alain. Jessica pressed the buzzer, and after a minute or two, a woman's voice asked, "Yes?"

Jessica took a deep breath. She was keeping her proposed scenario for their being there fixed firmly in her mind so she could pull the details out as needed.

"Hello. I'm Jessica Shepard. I'm with Alain Raynaud. We've met Louis Aspen already in Dalkey."

"Yes?"

"We were in Dublin and wondered if we might visit the office." She gave Alain a wink as she finished her breathless recital. He looked skeptical. But her planning was rewarded when, after a slight pause, she heard the voice on the other side of the buzzer answer.

"Oh all right. I guess so. Wait. I'll buzz you in."

The sound of the buzzer was feeble and brief, with some starts and stops, but it managed to resonate within the small, enclosed space of the foyer. And when Alain firmly turned the knob of the door, the catch released easily and they gained admittance, both almost surprised at their success. There was an elevator to their left and in front of them the inner door to Aspen Productions; it had a brass plaque, similar to the one on the outside of the building. They went inside the inner door and found a small office with a receptionist sitting behind a tiny, wooden desk.

"You know Mr. Aspen, do you?" she said immediately.

"Yes, we do," Jessica said. "You are?"

"I'm Peggy."

"Hello, Peggy."

"Hello. I work for Mr. Aspen—as his assistant here. He didn't mention that anyone would be stopping by. So at first, I was a little confused."

"No," Jessica said. "He wouldn't have mentioned us. You see, we were in Dublin and we thought we'd see what the office looks like. That's all."

"Oh. People do that from time to time, although I'm not sure why. I don't mind, but there really isn't much to see. I'm here most of the time by myself. I take the calls and sort the mail. Mr. Aspen is often out of the office. The only thing to look at, I guess, are the posters."

She pointed to the walls to the right and left of her, which had framed posters hanging on them. It seemed as though the boredom of working in an often deserted office was getting to her, and she was warming at the chance of having some personal interaction. Jessica wondered how often the characters on the large posters were Peggy's only companions.

"May I take a look?"

"Sure, suit yourself."

"Thanks." Jessica walked over to those on the left wall, then to those on the right. The posters all graphically represented titles and scenes of plays that had been produced by Aspen Productions; they had been played at various theaters in Dublin and other towns around Ireland. "I didn't know that Louis produced plays."

"He doesn't now—no more live theater, now only television—but before, he produced plays."

"Who's Beatrice Jones?" Alain asked.

Jessica took in all the posters as a whole. The posters had one thing in common. The same actress was depicted in all of them: Beatrice Jones. She appeared to be an attractive woman with long, dark hair and expressive features. She was prominently displayed in various costumes, depending on which play she was performing in for each poster.

"Oh, *Beatrice*." Peggy smiled and hesitated a moment, as though deciding how best to answer Alain's terse question. Then it seemed the temptation to combat loneliness by gossiping with a couple of infrequent visitors overcame her initial reticence about this particular subject. And she let loose like a pressure cooker suddenly relieved of its confining cover. "Beatrice and Mr. Aspen used to be quite an item. She was *discovered* by Mr. Aspen, and he liked to say that he 'cultivated her.'" She used the forefingers and middle fingers of each of her hands to put the last phrase in virtual quotation marks. Peggy's hands were becoming her most expressive props. Jessica wondered if, down the road, Louis rejoined the ranks of Dublin theater producers, whether there would be a place on the stage for his assistant, Peggy.

The girl's gregariousness continued growing. "She was in most of the plays the company produced. But then she had a falling out with Mr. Aspen."

"Oh really?" Jessica asked, getting more and more interested in Peggy's story line.

"I'm not sure exactly what the problems were. That's above my pay grade—at least for now." She laughed. "Anyway, once she left, Mr. Aspen sort of lost interest in live theater and the company moved on to television productions. I hadn't been working here that long before the switch happened, so I can't tell you much more. I'm happier with the television side of the business to tell you the truth. There's more variety. Things are always changing. The company seems to be pretty success-ful—at least from what I can see—if that's what you're worried about."

"Would you know how we could get in touch with Beatrice Jones?" Alain asked, treating Peggy to one of his most ingrati-ating smiles.

Peggy responded and said, "Sure." She immediately started clicking away at her computer. There were those expressive hands again, this time put to efficient use, and one more con-sistent with her current vocation. She came up with an address and telephone number almost instantly.

"She's in Dublin!" Jessica said triumphantly, looking over Alain's arm at the printout Peggy had just handed to him. Jessica now had her own ingratiating smile on display.

"Yes," Peggy said. "But it's not at home that you're likely to find her at today."

"Where would she be?" Jessica asked.

"You'll best find her near Meeting House Square at Temple Bar. She has a stand there most Saturdays. I've seen it myself. I'm only working a half day today, but I still have some things I've got to get done or I'd take you there myself. Even if for some reason she's not there, if you ask around, some of the other vendors might be able to let you know where she's hanging out."

"What does she do there?" Jessica asked.

"Beatrice paints all breeds of dogs, and she's quite good at it. The tourists—and even some locals—like to buy the one that's of the same breed as the dog they own. I guess it's eas-ier than getting your own dog to sit for a portrait—or even a photograph. My dog would never sit still for it. But I guess I'm not as good a dog trainer as Beatrice's turned out to be."

"That's quite a jump in professions. So she doesn't act anymore?" Jessica asked.

"Oh, I don't know about that. But at least not on Saturdays during the day. You can't miss her though. Just look for someone selling paintings only of dogs."

****

Jessica and Alain did not have far to walk from Aspen Productions to the heart of Temple Bar. Temple Bar was pedestrian friendly, chock-full with a mix of restaurants, shops, pubs, and bars. At that time of day, it was extremely crowded.

"I wonder if Peggy was overconfident about our ability to find Beatrice Jones among all these artisans making this place headquarters for all their stuff," Jessica said.

"Don't worry," Alain said as they threaded through the dense crowds. "We'll find her. There can't be more than one stall selling what Peggy described. By the way, are you going to be all right with a lot of pictures of dogs when we finally find her?" He was referring to Jessica's history of discomfort around the animals, which had been steadily improving with her determined effort to control it.

"Now *you* don't worry about that. No problem with the *painted* form."

"I'm happy to hear that."

"And as you know, that is *one* blemish on my credentials that has been getting smaller and smaller, Inspector Raynaud. But I do thank you for your concern!"

Jessica ignored his look of amusement and continued to assiduously scan the crowds. She looked right and left. All manner of items was displayed in different booths: pieces of silver jewelry, many including the classic Celtic Knot in their designs; porcelain and glass housewares; and knitted items of a selection of colors that rivalled the rainbow.

At last, she saw it. "There it is!" Jessica yelled out, causing a few of the pedestrians around her to turn their heads. "I have to watch my enthusiasm." She added in a lower pitch, "I'm startling the natives."

She pointed toward a booth composed of white sheeting on a metal rim. The back wall was hung with framed watercolor pictures of different breeds of dogs. All the frames were in the same size, so that the selection gave the illusion that one was staring into a kennel filled with live animals.

On the side of the booth were racks of unframed pictures, which were being arranged by a tall woman. She wore a lightweight, black, leather jacket with silver studs and a black, leather, paperboy cap with a brim with similar silver studs on it. Jessica immediately recognized her as the same woman who had graced the posters in Louis Aspen's production office. But the woman standing in the stall was now obviously older, and her costume was no longer that of any recognizable character in a play. She was wearing blue jeans and a T-shirt under her jacket. As they got closer, Jessica saw that across her chest, printed in black and white, was a sample reproduction of her artwork in the form of a King Charles spaniel. Jessica and Alain approached her.

"Beatrice Jones?" Jessica asked.

"Why yes. How can I help you?" She looked at them tentatively, as though Alain had subconsciously telegraphed his vocation in law enforcement and caused the woman to hesitate. But then Beatrice studied them, especially Jessica. And she seemed to relax and realize that it was more likely that the newcomers were just tourists. She asked, "Are you familiar with my work? That's gratifying to hear."

"Yes, we are, but perhaps not in the way you think," Jessica said.

Beatrice's tentative expression immediately returned. "I'm sorry. I don't think I understand you." She cast an even more bemused look at her potential new customers.

"No. I'm sorry. I don't mean to confuse you. My name is Jessica Shepard and—"

"Alain Raynaud," Alain interjected, simplifying Jessica's hesitancy at whether or not she should offer Alain's title, although she had automatically omitted her own.

Jessica continued speaking. "Let me explain why we sought you out. The two of us were approached by Louis Aspen and Michael Thornes about a possible television series of our own. We're aware you've worked with Louis in the past and thought it might be helpful to speak with you face-to-face about it."

"Louis is it?" She chuckled. "He gave you *my* name, did he?"

"Well, not directly."

"I figured not."

"No, we actually got your name from Peggy at Aspen Productions. We just came from there."

"No. I didn't think you'd get it from Louis. That's a fact. I guess you've both been subjected to some of Louis's charm, haven't you?"

"I guess you could say that."

Beatrice waited a minute while she scrunched up her forehead, as though thinking deeply on the spot about how much she should share with these two strangers. Then she bit her lip, shook her head slightly up and down as though coming to a decision, and said, "Yes. I worked with him in the past. But that was another chapter in my life. I've moved on. As you can see." She pointed to the backboard of her booth and the rack of pictures beside her.

Jessica had the weird sensation that all the dogs in their portraits were nodding heads with their vendor in silent agreement. "You know what?" Jessica asked. "Can we buy you something to drink? It's hot out here, and we would like to ask you about your experience working with him. It would be very helpful to us in reaching the best decision to pick your brain about what it was like. And it's only fair we make it a pleasant conversation. We can go into one of the pubs close by, if that's OK with you. We don't need to go very far. It shouldn't take long from your day. You choose where we go."

Beatrice bit her lip again. "Liam?" She suddenly called out to the young man in the stall right next to her. "Do you mind keeping an eye on my booth for the next half hour or so while I get something to drink with *my friends?* I'll make it up to you."

"Sure," Liam replied laconically, looking Jessica and Alain up and down quickly but studiously, as though memorizing their faces should Beatrice not return safely and he'd have to find a local policeman to file a missing person's report.

"Thanks," Beatrice said just as laconically, pulling down a corner of the stiff sheeting to cover her handiwork until she safely returned. "OK, *Jessica and Alain*, I'm all yours."

The three headed over to the closest pub. Inside was a long, narrow space that ran from front to back with open brickwork on its walls and wooden floors. The floors looked as though they had supported innumerable pairs of shoes that had trafficked over them. But the staff working the tables was friendly and obviously knew Beatrice by name. One of the staff pointed them to the back of the pub where they found an empty spot by the back door. Beatrice sat on one side of the varnished wooden table, across from Jessica and Alain. One face reflected against the other two on the highly polished surface, creating a portrait of sorts from the reflected light of a hanging lamp between them in the darkened interior of the pub.

"So what do you want to know?" Beatrice asked bluntly after three beers had been placed before them, the reflected portrait erased by the liquid that spilled on the table as the mugs were slammed down hard.

Jessica leaned forward. Her elbows were on the table, the fist of her left hand clasped in the palm of the other, tucked under her chin; it was the posture she would have assumed in didactic presentation during her prior years of training medical house staff. "Let me start by giving you some background to better understand why we approached you this way."

"I would appreciate that," Beatrice said.

"Yes. We owe you that. Louis Aspen does want to create a television series based lightly on Alain and my recent experiences. You see, Alain is a Canadian narcotics inspector—"

"I have nothing to do with drugs," Beatrice blurted out, causing at least a few heads in the pub to turn in their direction.

"We didn't think you did," Alain injected. "Don't worry. This has nothing to do with any of that."

"Well, I should hope not!" Beatrice added.

Jessica silenced Alain with her eyes and continued speaking to the other woman. "And I'm an immunologist. But the only reason we're mentioning our professions is to explain that the two of us have been involved recently in the solution of several murder cases in which our professions played roles in helping to solve them."

Beatrice's eyes widened and she paled slightly. But she remained silent, allowing Jessica to go on without any further interruptions. "So that's what interested Aspen and Thornes. It gave them ideas for some plots for the series."

"I see," Beatrice said, narrowing her eyes.

"Anyway, Alain and I met with them both in Dalkey at an inn there—Castle Ryan. Have you heard of it, by the way?"

"No. I don't think so, at least not that I can remember."

"OK. Let me provide some more background."

"That would be helpful."

Jessica ignored the former actress's intonation and continued speaking. "Many years ago, there was a suspicious death at the castle. The deceased was *the lady of the manor.* I guess one would call her that. Then, just while I've been staying there, a writer, who was also a guest, expired from an overdose of sleeping pills."

"I would think it would be the police that would investigate that. I still don't see why you're telling me about it."

"Don't get me wrong. They are. Of course. But this second death was somewhat unusual."

"More unusual than an overdose of sleeping pills?"

"Yes, in a way."

"How so?"

"You see the woman who died was found dressed similarly to the well-known costume of the other woman who died there all those years ago. That's what made it seem more unusual."

Beatrice's pallor suddenly returned and spread from her forehead to her neck. She took a long drink of beer. Her voice box moved visibly up and down in her long neck as she swallowed the draught. The alcohol accomplished its task and brought back some color to her face. "Now I understand," she finally said. "Look, I'm not saying anything that people who worked with me when I was in the theater don't already know. So I guess there's no harm in sharing it. But maybe no one in television knows about it."

"About what?" Jessica blurted out.

Beatrice bit her lip one more time and then took another swig of beer before continuing. "Louis liked to drum up publicity. He felt it was a crucial part of the process. He felt it helped to drive ticket sales. He was probably right. People can be ghoulish, can't they? Well, to make a long story short, the last character I played got strangled during a robbery in the final act. So following a logical train of thought, what do you think Louis did, as only he could?"

Jessica and Alain remained silent. Neither of them wanted to interrupt her narrative at this stage in the game.

Beatrice shook her head, as though still unable to believe what she was about to say. Then she looked directly at Jessica and Alain. "He had arranged to have someone strangle me!"

"You must be joking," Jessica blurted out again.

"I wish I were," Beatrice said quietly. "Oh, not to hurt me, mind you. Just strangle me enough to get it in the local paper in the town where the play was running at the time—like he wanted to try it out on an audience—see how it went over with the crowds, you might say. Well, I got wind of the plan before he got very far." She laughed bitterly. "He tried to use a local punk who got scared stiff at the very last minute. Then the word got out—finally even to *me*, fool that I was. Well, that was enough! That was the final straw—whatever you want to call it. I decided to take some time off, spend some time with my dog. *At least a dog you can trust.*"

Jessica ignored Alain's barely perceptible smile at Beatrice's last line.

"Anyway, I started painting my dog, and then I came up with the idea to paint all different dog breeds. Why not? I liked doing it. It made me happy. And you know what? I found out that people like buying the ones that match the breeds of their own dogs. Isn't that funny? It's almost like it's a family portrait, but without the bother of getting the dog to sit for the painting. I'm doing all right for myself. The gig pays the rent and keeps food on the table—with a lot less heartache than the theater, I might add."

Beatrice took one more swig of beer. "Listen, don't get me wrong. Louis isn't that bad a guy really. He isn't when compared to some others I've known. At least, he wasn't when I knew him. I think he just sort of lost his way. I guess that's not so *unusual*—at least, not like the deaths that you've mentioned today. Maybe he's now the way he was when I first met him. He did have his romantic side at times." She was silent, and for just a moment her eyes seemed to mist over. "He used to say he was my Dante and I was his Beatrice. Ah well, I guess time passes, doesn't it? But I'm not one to allow myself to get sentimental. That's not a good thing to be. I've learned that." She looked up from her mug of beer that was now practically empty.

Alain asked, "Did the police ever get involved with any of this?"

"Oh no. It never got very far, as I said. No one got hurt. Certainly not me—at least, not physically. *Emotionally*—now that's another issue. But anyway, after that I decided to leave the theater. I had had enough but didn't want to be vengeful. I just wanted to get on with my life. I thought it was the best thing for me to do."

"It sounds like you have done that," Jessica said. "But you've given us a lot to think about. And we thank you for that and for all your honesty. It's been very helpful."

"Well, look, I had better get back to my stall. Liam will start getting worried, and believe me: that wouldn't be good for either of *you*. Now *he's* a good sort of chap if we're doing a survey. Unfortunately, he's married. Anyway, thanks for the drink and good luck to you both, whatever you decide to do." Beatrice got up from the table and walked shakily out of the pub. She didn't look back at either of them until she was out the door.

"So what do you think about what she said, Alain?"

"I think we should get back to Dalkey and try to figure out if Aspen, for whatever reason, tried a similar plan out a second time, but with more success on repeat."

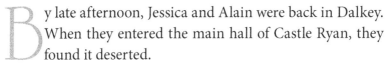

Sixteen
The Story Continues
in Dalkey

By late afternoon, Jessica and Alain were back in Dalkey. When they entered the main hall of Castle Ryan, they found it deserted.

"I guess Frankie's death has taken its toll on the potential clientele of the castle," Jessica said as she looked around the empty space.

"Bad news travels fast," Alain said.

Jessica could guess how quickly the word had gotten around; the community was tight.

They sat down in a corner of the hall to plan what next steps they should take. Ensconced in one of the two side-by-side, high-backed, upholstered chairs, Jessica might have been lulled into somnolence by the soft cushioning if it wasn't for the metal shield, with the coat of arms of Castle Ryan on it, which was shining out of a display case to the right of their chairs. The shield served to keep her on her game. Surprisingly, it was the first time she had noticed the shield in the room. But from the size of the case, it was clear that the coat of arms would not be easily moved, and it must have been there all along. But she had never bothered to investigate that corner of the hall.

She finally turned her head to remove the bright metal from her line of vision and said, "Alain, before we speak again with Louis and Michael, why don't we see if anyone here had any deeper connection with Frankie that wasn't obvious to me or that we've come upon so far?"

"You don't like going in a straight line, do you?"

"Well, no, I guess I don't. But maybe proceeding my way can shed some light on whether Frankie used pills to sleep in the past. I'm uncomfortable confronting Louis only based on Beatrice's tip. I'd prefer to start with a tabula rasa."

"That's you. I usually prefer to start with the most likely lead and go on from there."

"I know you do. But I'm so used to the process of differential diagnosis: ruling out other possibilities before settling on the most likely one. I'd just like to be sure once we go down a particular path that we haven't missed one less likely. I'm OK with excluding those we should exclude, just as long as we don't go too far down one way—with blinders on—and make a mistake."

"Fine. Understood. But who do you have in mind that we should focus on?"

"I was thinking of Stanley Bogart. Maybe he could give us some leads. He's a piano composer who seemed to have had a bit of a thing for Frankie. *Then* there's also Joel Ryan, the Ryans' son."

"Why him?"

"Only that his sister, Alice, told me he was a crime story fan. That could be a possible connection to Frankie. Crime fiction was her genre. They had that appreciation in common. I know it's a thin link, but it's a link in the chain just the same."

"Sounds reasonable to me. Which one do you want to start with? I'm open to either one. I'll let you choose."

Jessica thought a moment and then said, "Stanley. Yes, Stanley. Let's start with him."

****

Jessica led Alain down to the lower level of the castle and to the baby grand piano, which was still set up just outside the conference room. As expected, Stanley was also there, morosely pounding away on the piano keys. His back was curved over the keyboard in as desultory a position as Jessica had yet seen him display. He was alone.

"Hello, Stanley," Jessica said.

Stanley looked up from the keyboard with glazed eyes.

Jessica wasn't sure he had heard her. So she asked more loudly, "Can we speak with you?"

"Sure, why not?" he finally said. "I've got nothing but time *now.*"

It seemed a good idea to use the conference room to talk, although in the state Stanley was in, they would have been able to lead him anywhere. He was totally passive, as if he couldn't direct his body by himself. They settled him at one of the tables in the empty room. Jessica was unsure as she talked to him if her explanation of why they wanted to speak was registering at all. The table was too large for only three people; they were bunched at one end of it. The massive dimensions of the room and the empty tables around them swallowed them up, but at least it seemed sure that no one would interrupt their conversation.

As Alain began speaking to Stanley, Jessica hoped the brusque detective would tailor his often intimidating manner to one less threatening for someone not used to it. Stanley's movements were slow and his verbal responses hesitant, both modulations of his prior demeanor and likely the posttraumatic effects of Frankie's recent death. Alain laboriously explained his credentials, why he was in Dalkey, and his connection to Jessica in the past and currently.

Finally, Alain said, "I know you might have answered some of these questions for the authorities, but Jessica and I were also curious if you knew if Frankie had a habit of using sleeping pills."

Stanley eyed Jessica and Alain and appeared satisfied that the question was not implicating him. It was the first time he seemed to display any caginess, and this new demeanor surprised Jessica.

Then he emphatically said, "No. Definitely not!" He hesitated and then added, "You must know she wasn't interested in me. At least, not in any way I wanted her to be."

"I'll agree she seemed distant in that respect," Jessica said.

"Yes, *distant*. But I thought we understood each other, despite the lack of closeness otherwise. She granted me that. No. I can say with assurance that it wasn't her *habit*. I certainly can't imagine why she would start on that particular night of all nights."

"Could she have been under some type of stress?" Jessica asked.

"Well, she was working on a new book. But she never mentioned any problems with extra stress affecting her sleep—at least not to me."

Jessica leaned over closer to Stanley. "If Frankie did use them without your knowing, do you have any idea where she would have gotten them—or from whom?"

"No. Except from a doctor, I guess. The only doctor who has any connection to this place is Dev Matthews, from what I know."

"Yes, I met him the night of the party."

"But he takes care of Brenda's knee and Amy Stanwich's complaints. And I can't believe someone as independent as Frankie was would have gotten them from the likes of him." He harrumphed. It was clear the pianist did not hold with the concept of total trust in a local generalist.

"Well, you never know," Alain said. "That's a connection we'll have to look into, in any case." He shot a sideways glance at Jessica, as though from long habit of having a subordinate partner on a case he expected her to jot the name down in a notebook to have on hand to scan later at his convenience.

"Look," Stanley added.

"Yes?" Alain drawled out.

"Don't say I mentioned anything. I told you I can't believe Frankie would have gotten them from him."

"All right, we won't. Jessica, is there anything else you want to ask Stanley?"

"No. I don't think so." She could see that Stanley looked like he had no intention of saying anything more, no matter what she wanted. "We'll let you get back to your composing."

"Yes. Thank you for that. I'm working on a piece that I'm going to dedicate to Frankie's memory. She was my muse, you know, even if she was a distant one."

****

Jessica and Alain next located Joel Ryan. The son of the castle's proprietors was busy arranging towels for any guest who might wish to use one of the exercise machines in the spa. Jessica knew she wouldn't be using one for the pool any time soon. Now that she had come to know the Ryans better, she could more clearly see that Joel was, although younger, almost a carbon copy of his father. Even the son's slenderer form would likely fill out to perfectly resemble that of his father's bulkier physique.

Once again, Alain explained that he and Jessica were seeking to learn a few details about Frankie's death. He tailored his monologue to the younger man's different relationship to the deceased woman than the one the pianist had had with her.

"I'm not sure I can tell you anything more than the police already know," Joel said, skepticism dripping from his tongue despite Alain's valiant effort to engage him.

"Well, you never know," Alain said, those words seeming to become his new motto. "Why don't you try?"

"And I'm not sure that I should even be speaking about it." Joel looked back and forth at Alain and Jessica as he might at his father and mother to determine which of them was the more sympathetic party to address his reservations.

"I understand your reticence," Alain said. He waited a moment and then added, "Jessica heard from your sister, Alice, that you're a crime fiction fan. Is that true?"

A smile suddenly flashed across Joel's lips. It was as though a pleasure switch had been turned on and lit the young man up. He looked to each side of him, as if to assure himself that no one would be needing a towel in the near future. Then he said with a conspiratorial air, which he might have pirated from one of those very same crime books, "Come into the office. We can talk better in there. If someone comes by, they can always ring the bell on the desk and I'll come back out."

He took Jessica and Alain into a tiny office behind his station at the castle's spa. It had just enough room for the three of them to squeeze into without much excess breathing space. He sat down behind the small metal desk, leaving Jessica and Alain to take the two empty chairs across from him. He seemed to suddenly enjoy being in charge of the conversation, again displaying a conspiratorial bend as he leaned forward closer to them.

"I do love crime fiction. That's what Frankie wrote."

"Yes, we know that," Jessica said.

"Yes, you would already know that, I guess. But that's the main reason that Frankie liked to stay at the castle when she was starting a new story. She told me that the setting was good for her. She said she got 'the right vibrations' for the types of books she wrote when she was here. She told me it was as though the castle itself got her *creative juices* flowing through her veins."

"Did she ever mention to you any difficulty sleeping or the need to take pills to sleep?" Jessica asked.

"No. She never did. We just always talked about what ideas she had for the plots for her books. Sometimes she would ask me what I thought about an idea she had—did it ring true or not? Just things like that. Nothing more."

"Did she ever show you any of her writings?" Alain asked.

"No. Never. She was funny that way. She never minded *talking* to me. But she was very private about what she *wrote* down. She said she never used a computer until she had the story all worked out on paper. She needed to look at her paper notes as she wrote the first draft. That way it was easier for her to make sure she wasn't getting off the right track of her crime stories. She liked to flip the pages back and forth that way to check things out as she wrote the additions, comparing them with what she'd already written. So that way there weren't any inconsistencies."

"So she never used a computer?" Alain asked.

"Only when she was totally finished working out the plot would she computerize it. She was always very cagey about her writings when she was just beginning them."

For a few minutes, Joel seemed to be thinking, and then he looked directly at Jessica and Alain and said, "You know, I didn't think about it before, but I don't think anyone said what happened to her notebooks."

"Wouldn't the police have taken them?" Jessica asked.

"Yeah, you'd think so, but I don't think the notebooks were in her room. You see, we use rotating daily staff to clean the rooms. I think I remember Alice saying Frankie asked about that—like it worried her. Like she didn't trust a stranger coming into her room if her notebooks were there."

Jessica thought a moment and then said, "Do you have a safe for valuables? Might she have placed them in there?"

"We do have one, but I don't handle that part of the business. Only my ma and Alice do."

"Why don't we talk to your mother?" Alain said.

****

Brenda leaned over Castle Ryan's safe and turned the knob slowly and carefully, back and forth on the ancient-looking device, while she silently mouthed the combination numbers. Her lips moved ever so slightly as she mentally recalled the numbers. It appeared she would have taken the task as seriously if she were performing it at a heavily guarded bank vault. She interrupted her task momentarily to throw a commentary over her right shoulder to her son who was just behind her.

"Frankie interrupted me so many times—making me take her notebooks out and then put them back in again. It became second nature to me, so much so that I never thought about it while I was doing it. Now that I'm thinking about it, somehow it seems harder and I can't remember for the life of me if the last time I handled them I was putting them in or taking them out!"

"We'll see soon enough, Ma, once you *finally* open the safe," Joel said, obviously beginning to struggle with impatience at the length of time his mother was taking to pop open the safe.

"All right! All right! I'm not as young as you are—or as I once was—now am I?"

"I'm not saying anything more, Ma."

"Well, don't. Just wait until you're my age, and with my bad knee and all, and you'll see what it's like. There!"

Triumph was evident in the glance she threw back at her son as the click she was waiting for echoed through the back room. She pulled open the thick, heavy door to the safe with some effort and looked deep inside.

Close at hand, just behind her back, were Joel, Jessica, and Alain. It had taken all of Joel's persuasive qualities to convince his mother that it was appropriate to open the safe and peek inside to see if Frankie's notebooks were there. He had cornered her behind the reception desk, enticing her to let Jessica and Alain come with them into the back office to take a look.

This room was much larger than the one dedicated to Joel in the spa. It was evident the familial hierarchy of the running of Castle Ryan was telegraphed by the business space delegated to each family member. The room was well lit and had a large wooden desk and several filing cabinets scattered about it. The safe was positioned against the back wall. Brenda steadied herself by holding on to the top of the safe and pulled out a couple of small cases, setting them on the desk. And then she reached again into the safe to rub her hand across all surfaces of the interior cube.

"It's not here! I'm sorry, Joel."

"Damn!" Joel said.

"Now don't curse," Brenda admonished.

The treasure hunt atmosphere had somehow managed to penetrate even her, and disappointment was clear in the sound of her voice. She placed a maternal hand on her son's shoulder. "Well, that settles it for me. Now I remember. The last time she asked me to go to the safe it must have been to take *out* her notebooks. Yes, I do remember. It was the day of the party. I was so distracted with all the preparations that were going on, and I was in such an enormous hurry. She said she had some ideas that she was afraid she would forget, so she didn't want to wait until her usual writing hours the next day for me to open the safe for her."

"But then where are the notebooks if they're not in the safe and they weren't in her room?" Jessica said, her own disappointment raising the pitch of her question a full octave higher.

"Well, I don't know about that," Brenda said. "But I'm sure they weren't in her room, now that I think back, because I remember exactly what they looked like. Also, Alice would have noticed them even if I hadn't. They weren't there that night. I'm sure of it."

"Maybe she hid them in the room somewhere no one noticed?" Jessica persisted.

"No, the police went over that room and showed me the list of what they found to see if I noticed anything that was out of the ordinary. And nothing was. I just didn't think about the notebooks then. Again, I'm sorry."

"They have to be somewhere unless she destroyed them," Alain said

"Oh, she would never have done that!" Joel said. "Like I said, she never computerized them until she was done working out her plot. And she always told everyone the minute she finished one. She would be so happy with that accomplishment."

"Yes," Brenda agreed. "She was so proud of reaching that point. If she was at the castle when she did, she'd always tell anyone who would listen that she had worked everything out. She never said much before that point though. It was as if she didn't want anyone telling her what to do—as if she didn't want to be influenced in any way by anyone else."

"Except for me, Ma," Joel said proudly.

"That's right. Except for Joel here, of course. She'd ask him, but only if things that she'd written were plausible or not, and then only at the very end. Isn't that right, Joel?" She looked at her son, who nodded vigorously.

"Well, I think we've reached a *dead end*," Jessica said plaintively.

"Now don't be discouraged," Brenda said, her maternal instincts on full display. "A bright young lady like you and this intelligent man here with you, why you'll both figure something out. I'm sure of it."

"Too bad we didn't come across a deux ex machina, like Frankie would have probably written in to one of her books," Jessica added.

"No, I don't think we need a contrived plot device, and I don't think we've reached a dead end either," Alain said. "At least, not yet. But now we know that if the notebooks weren't destroyed, and it sounds like that's unlikely—at least by the author—someone else has them. And before we can figure out who does, we need to learn more about how Frankie ended up incapacitated that night. Because it's almost certain the two events are interconnected."

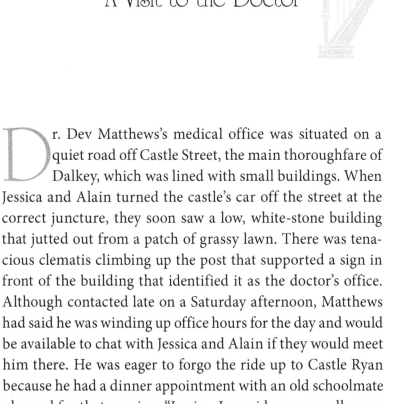

Seventeen
A Visit to the Doctor

D r. Dev Matthews's medical office was situated on a quiet road off Castle Street, the main thoroughfare of Dalkey, which was lined with small buildings. When Jessica and Alain turned the castle's car off the street at the correct juncture, they soon saw a low, white-stone building that jutted out from a patch of grassy lawn. There was tenacious clematis climbing up the post that supported a sign in front of the building that identified it as the doctor's office. Although contacted late on a Saturday afternoon, Matthews had said he was winding up office hours for the day and would be available to chat with Jessica and Alain if they would meet him there. He was eager to forgo the ride up to Castle Ryan because he had a dinner appointment with an old schoolmate planned for that evening. "Jessica, I consider you a colleague, even though our specialties are different—you, an immunologist, and I, a generalist—so I am happy to accommodate you," he had said.

Jessica and Alain entered the vestibule of the office and smelled the biting odor of disinfectant, which must have been used recently to wipe down the surfaces of the exam rooms. The smell permeated from the inner rooms of the medical suite and lingered by the door to the outside; what air had been brought in as they entered failed to dilute it. Jessica wrinkled up her nose but thought the odor a reassuring sign that the doctor's medical practice took infection control seriously; that, at least, contradicted Stanley Bogart's quick dismissal of the country doctor's expertise.

No patients remained in the office. And there was no receptionist at the small, wooden desk by the entrance door. Jessica called out, "Dr. Matthews? Dr. Matthews?" She turned to Alain. "I hope he hasn't left and forgot to lock the door. Even if he is somewhere in the back of the suite, he should have been able to hear us." Despite her eagerness to do so, it didn't seem ethical to forage for where he might be.

But a few minutes later, an inner door opened and the doctor came out to greet them.

"Hello. Hello," he said.

"Hello, Dr. Matthews. Is this still a good time to speak?" Jessica asked.

"Yes, of course, it is or I wouldn't have told you to drop by. But I appreciate your being on time. My patients rarely do so. They tend to come too early or too late and then complain about having to wait."

"Well, we appreciate you making the time to talk," Alain said.

"That's not a problem. Come back into my consultation room. I've been waiting for you. But I was reading through some charts and must have gotten lost in thought because I didn't hear you both come in until you called out to me." He extended his arm back to his inner sanctum with a gesture that had likely been performed many times to many patients over his years in medical practice. "There are three chairs there, and we can sit and talk undisturbed. As you can see, we are alone now. My receptionist and nurse left shortly after I was done with my last patient. They were eager to get out and begin their evenings. As I told you, I also can't give you much time because I have a dinner appointment. It was a busy day, although you wouldn't guess it from looking at the office now. I am tired, but I'm looking forward to a relaxing dinner."

He led them into the room and sat down behind his desk, motioning for Jessica and Alain to take the two chairs across from him.

"We also appreciate you making yourself available on such short notice, busy as you are," Jessica said. "Have you practiced here long?"

"Oh, now it feels like all my life."

"I bet it does," Jessica agreed.

"Yes. And I'm sure when I see my former school friend tonight and I get a good look at how he's aged—and he gets a good look at me—I'll feel it even more acutely. You see, I started here soon after I completed my training. And once I got my feet wet in this practice, somehow I never wanted to go anywhere else. I don't think that's so uncommon."

"No, I guess not," Jessica said.

"Well, there's a history around these parts and I enjoy that. It gives one a feeling of permanence despite the passing of years. My, how I'm sounding. I must be more tired from the day's work than I first thought. Now I'm sure you both haven't come to my office only to learn about my life story, unless, Dr. Shepard—Jessica—you're thinking of relocating here."

"No, nothing like that."

"No, I didn't really think that. But you said there was something in particular you wanted to ask me about. So how can I help you?" He looked over the top of his spectacles at Jessica and then at Alain. He was now seemingly focused, sitting back in what must be his usual manner behind his consultation desk. He no longer appeared aware of his own fatigue.

"Obviously, we were both very disturbed about what happened to Frankie Alexis," Jessica said.

"Yes, very sad, very sad," Matthews said.

"I was especially affected because I knew her personally," Jessica continued. "Although it was only for the short time that we came in contact with each other at Castle Ryan where we were both staying."

"Of course. Yes. So unfortunate an event. And she was so talented. I don't know if you've read any of her work."

"No, I haven't."

"She hadn't published much yet. But she would have, and what she had published so far was actually very good. At least, I think so. Although her genre isn't really my favorite. Spy stories are more my cup of tea. But each to his own as they say, as long as it's done well."

"Were you aware of her using sleeping pills?" Alain interjected, curtailing any further literary panegyrics to the now deceased, crime-story writer.

Jessica knew Alain still didn't hold much agreement with her circular style of getting at what she wanted to know but preferred being more direct in his questioning. She could see he was impatient to bring the doctor back on track.

Alain's question though must have hit home because Matthews did not appear to take any offense at Alain's inflection and immediately said, "Yes. I must confess that I wondered if that was really what you wanted to know when you both asked to come over—especially when the cause of death became known."

"It would be helpful," Jessica now interjected.

"I don't mind answering the question." Matthews turned to Alain. "The local police also asked me about it. They also checked the pharmacist's records, I believe. I imagine they would have been derelict in their duty to the case if they hadn't. But the answer is *no*. To my knowledge, she didn't use them. And I certainly didn't prescribe them to her. You see, I only use them sparingly, and even then, mainly for little old ladies, like my old friend Amy Stanwich." He looked back at Jessica. "And I only mention *that* because I remember her saying it during our introduction, Jessica, on that fateful night. So rest assured that if the unfortunate Frankie took too many pills, intentionally or unintentionally, believe me: she didn't get them from me or from my office."

****

"Well, I guess even with our best efforts we're no closer than we were before," Jessica said, disappointment creeping into her voice.

"I wouldn't say that," Alain said.

"Why not? I made you satisfy my desire for following the rules of differential diagnosis. And I don't think it got us anywhere at all."

She was sitting next to Alain in the car they had taken to get to Matthews's office. They were pulled off the road and halfway back to the castle so they could speak in private, having left the doctor at his office to close up for the evening and his anticipated dinner. The yellow gorse by the side of the road at that time of beginning nightfall was casting an eerie, sallow glow over the ground; it shone against the deepening darkness of the sky. Jessica looked out the car window, letting a deep sigh escape her before opening the window to allow some of the cool, refreshing breeze to hit her face.

"Don't be discouraged. Negative information is just as helpful as positive information. You should know that. If none of the people around her knew Frankie to be one to take sleeping pills—and it seems the ones we've spoken to so far knew her fairly well and said she didn't—it makes it less likely that she would have them and make her own mistake or not with an overdose."

"That's true." Jessica looked back at Alain. "Also, there's those missing notebooks. They really bother me." Jessica bit at her rough thumbnail as if the tactile gesture would help her to think more clearly and successfully arrange the many tangled threads of facts they had before them. But she was nowhere close to having them all rolled into a neat, tidy skein. "You know, when I arrived and met Frankie for the first time on the patio of the castle, I remember her furiously scribbling in one. Her notebooks must have been so precious to her. Just look at how she used to lock them up in the safe as another woman might lock up her jewelry."

Jessica then presented her right hand to Alain, positioning her wrist practically under his nose. "By the way, what do you think of this jet bracelet?"

He pulled her hand down and turned her wrist over in his hands so that her palm was facing up toward the roof of the car. For a moment it struck her that he might kiss it, but he rubbed her wrist with his thumb, smiled, and said, "Very nice indeed."

She was not disappointed because the smile seemed as valuable as a kiss. "Thank you. I bought it at a local antiques shop. Anyway, my point is if I wanted to keep it safe, I certainly wouldn't leave it lying around so anyone could find it. Frankie obviously felt the same way about her notebooks. She locked them up whenever she wasn't writing in them. She also wouldn't have just left them lying around so anyone could take them—and especially not before a big party when there was likely to be so many people around the castle who might not usually be there."

"So then what do you think she did with them?"

"Well, we know Frankie used to jot down her ideas in the notebooks as soon as possible, before the train of thought left her. And we know she had Brenda remove them from the safe that night so she could do just that. Frankie obviously never got a chance to get her notebooks back to the safe. And if she didn't hide them anywhere else that we haven't found yet, I think someone gave her sleeping pills, and whoever did that also pinched her notebooks while she was out of commission."

"Pinched?"

"Yes, *pinched*. I believe it's the proper word for what must have happened, Inspector!"

"Fair enough. We won't quibble any longer about terminology."

"Thank you!"

"So you believe what was in those notebooks was important enough that it was worth murdering Frankie to get it?"

"Well, I know that seems improbable, but maybe the whole thing was some type of big mistake. Maybe she got more pills than she was supposed to get. I just don't know."

Alain was silent for a moment and then said, "You might be onto something after all."

"Thank you again. I'm flattered that you agree."

"You're welcome. Anyway, I think it is now time to talk to Louis Aspen before we do anything further. We need to follow back on what Beatrice Jones told us while we were in Dublin. Maybe using her lead, we'll get some more information out of him. Why don't we take that direct path you're so against? Let's get back to the castle and get on with it."

Eighteen
The Screenwriter Is
Found; the Producer Isn't

Jessica and Alain returned to Castle Ryan only to learn that Louis Aspen was out for the evening; any attempt to speak with him would have to wait until the following day. They had more luck finding Michael Thornes. The screenwriter was ensconced in the library, enjoying a tidy cocktail when Jessica and Alain walked in on him.

"Hello. Good evening," he said, looking up at them and putting his martini glass onto the side table by his club chair.

Jessica and Alain sat down across from him. Jessica thought that without his partner, the man looked more at ease. But maybe it was the martini glass that was doing the trick.

"Will you have one?" he asked, picking up the glass again and raising it up with one hand in front of him like a trophy for presentation. He picked the olive out of the glass with the other hand and popped the stone fruit into his mouth with relish.

"That sounds like a very good idea," Alain answered. "Jessica?" He looked to his side and received a brief nod from her. It wasn't her favorite drink. But somehow it seemed to fit the mark as the urbane drink for the occasion, especially if they wanted to follow the image Michael was apparently projecting while his partner was absent. So she didn't demur by requesting another kind of cocktail.

Thornes immediately stood up, taking the cue as he might have a stage direction written into one of his screenplays. "Let me go find Lora. The girl was just here a few minutes ago. She should be close at hand. I'll ask her to bring in two more. Mine was made well. Surprisingly so." He left through the library door. The sound of his shoes hitting the heavy flagstones of the floor of the main hall echoed with diminishing strength while he walked away from the library.

"Well, he seemed more gregarious than he has been so far," Jessica said as soon as they could no longer hear Thornes's footsteps outside the library. "Time to switch gears, I guess, and settle on him for answering questions. He's all we've got. But I'm still disappointed we couldn't find Louis tonight."

"I wouldn't be disappointed. Thornes may know as much as Aspen—and he may be even more likely to talk openly if Aspen isn't around. Aspen seems to monopolize the conversation whenever the two are together. Thornes is a writer, isn't he? He should be very interested in talking if given the chance. Words are part and parcel of his craft."

"That's true."

"And who knows? What we have to discuss might give him some ideas for his next screenplay."

"Was that sarcasm?"

"Perhaps a little."

"Good. I read you correctly. But we don't know how long he's been working with Louis. He may know nothing about what Beatrice Jones told us. We may just be wasting our time here."

"But I thought you liked differential diagnosis. Anyway, he may know more than we think. He could have crossed paths with Frankie Alexis in some way that we don't know of—and even know something about her notebooks."

"So now you feel the same way about them as I do?"

"How so?"

"That there's something important about those notebooks, rather than just a crime writer's personal notes."

"Yes. I told you that you may be right on that score. *Ssh.* Here he's coming back."

Thornes was at the library door. "I was successful. I found Lora. She's coming by shortly with two fresh martinis for the two of you." He entered the room and sat down again in the chair opposite Jessica and Alain.

"Thank you for taking the trouble," Jessica said. "Michael, I wanted to ask how long you have been a screenwriter."

"Oh, at least ten years now, I would say."

"Have you been working with Louis exclusively all that time?"

"No. Only for about the past two years. Why? Are you both still on the fence about Louis's project? You're both sure taking your time about it. You're lucky Louis is a determined man, or he might have walked out already."

"Well, these decisions do take some time," Jessica said. "You must understand that. Also, I've been so unsettled about what happened to Frankie Alexis."

"Yes, that was very tragic. Yes, *tragic.* That's the word for it. Almost makes one want to get up and run away from this place, doesn't it? But I guess it's unfair to blame the castle for the things its guests do."

"Yes." Jessica paused a moment. Then seeing that, at least for the present, Alain was content to allow her to proceed in her own roundabout way, she continued. "Frankie was a writer— like yourself."

"A screenwriter?" He looked at her, slightly puzzled.

"No. I didn't mean that exactly. She wrote crime thrillers."

"Oh, I see. Well, I've not read her work."

"Apparently she was working on a new book."

"Is that so?"

"Yes. She was writing a good deal while she was here. I don't know if you noticed that. She was always scribbling away whenever I saw her. Also, what's interesting is that we've learned that some of her notebooks, which she was writing in so assiduously, have gone missing."

"Really? Now that is interesting. Well, that's the castle's responsibility, I would think, rather than yours or mine."

"So she never spoke to you about them?"

"The notebooks? No. Not at all."

"Louis didn't always only work in television, did he? He used to be involved in theater work, didn't he?"

"Sorry, I can't tell you much about that. As I said, I've only worked with him for about the past two years, and only in television. Not in any other medium."

He drained his martini glass and stood up, almost knocking over the glass that he had placed on the edge of the table next to his chair. He caught it with both hands and righted it successfully. Then he stood back up, clearly indicating that their tête-à-tête was nearing its culmination.

"Again, I wish I could help. Although I'm not really sure why you're both interested in all this. Oh, sorry. I forgot you're onto your next case." He laughed. But somehow it struck Jessica that he didn't manage to exude the confidence Louis would have been able to show. It seemed as though Michael noticed that for himself and he said, "Louis will like that. Anyway, I would advise you both to finalize your decision about the project we discussed. Louis is very excited about it, and of course, so am I. But at some point, we may need to move on."

He bid them good night and left the library.

"Thanks for letting me go about it in my own way," Jessica said once she was sure they were alone again.

"You did a good job."

"You think so?"

"Yes. Definitely. Also, it gave me the chance to watch him while you asked him questions."

"What do you think about him?" Jessica asked, although she had her own thoughts as she gestured toward the door to the library through which Michael had exited.

"I think he knows a lot more than he's letting on."

"I do too," she said firmly.

****

"We've just got to get into Michael's room," Jessica said the next morning. They were again sitting in the two chairs by Castle Ryan's coat of arms and using the area as their place of business to plan next steps. "I wonder if we can get Joel to help us. He was willing to help us before."

"What makes you so sure that if Thornes had those notebooks, he'd leave them in his room? Frankie Alexis didn't, so why would he? It was your reasoning. And remember we still don't know if we'll find anything helpful in them in the first place."

"Call it woman's intuition if you want to. I just have a hunch about it. It was the way he reacted when we mentioned them. He looked so nervous."

"OK, I'll grant you that. And far be it from me to criticize your intuition. I have to admit that it's been true in the past. So I'll go along with you on this one. Anyway, we have nothing to lose. Why don't we go find our young crime fiction fan and see if he'll be as helpful as you think he'll be?"

They again located Joel outside the castle's spa. He was still counting out towels. A quick look at the young man told Jessica how very bored he was as he loyally performed tasks not nearly as adventurous as his eager spirit demanded. He was tossing each clean, white towel quickly down onto the others in an ever-growing pile; irritation was evident in every exaggerated flick of his strong wrist.

"Hello, Joel," Jessica said.

"Hello." He finally looked up from the towels and seemed to focus slowly on Jessica and Alain.

"Joel, we need your help."

"My help?" Joel sharpened up even more.

"Yes. We have a little caper we need your help with."

"Caper, heh?"

"Yes, we need to get into another guest's room with your assistance—the one Michael Thornes has."

Without any hesitation, Joel said, "I think we need an accomplice. And I don't mean my mother this time." He pulled out his cell phone, entered a number, and a few moments later, they heard him say authoritatively into the phone, "Alice, it's me." He then launched into a set of detailed instructions. These were relayed to his sister with an ease as worthy as it would be if the siblings were planning to pilfer nuclear secrets from a secure database rather than merely getting into Michael Thornes's vacated hotel room. Joel finished speaking and popped off his cell phone. Then he looked up at Jessica and Alain. And with a broad grin spreading over his face, he said, "She's all in on *my* plan!"

****

Alice was upstairs on the landing that loomed over the main hall and led to the wing in which Thornes's guest room was located. It was the wing opposite to the one Jessica's, Frankie's, and Stanley's rooms were housed. "This is more fun than dressing up that silly owl," Alice whispered to her brother. She turned to Jessica and Alain and continued whispering. "Ma and Pop don't know anything about what we're doing, so we have to be super quiet so the beans aren't spilled. Ma has ears everywhere. She's very impressive that way. I told Mr. Thornes and Mr. Aspen—his room's just next to Mr. Thornes's—that when one of the staff was cleaning, she found some ants and I'm having the exterminator in to take care of the problem."

"Ma won't like that one, Alice," Joel chuckled.

"I know. Tell me about it. Ma will probably freak when she hears of it! But it's the best tale I could come up with on such short notice. Anyway, both men are on the patio now having Sunday brunch. And I have Lora on duty there, to keep them waiting for their food and their bill until I give her the all-clear to let them leave. Don't worry. That's all Lora knows, just to do that, nothing more. Luckily, she's not a particularly curious person. But she'll warn me if she can't stall them any longer. So we have to work quickly, mind you."

The group of four quietly slipped down the hall. They passed the room that was Alain's and then continued on to those of Thornes and Aspen. Alice opened Thornes's room with her key, and they piled in after her, closing the door securely behind them.

Jessica looked around her and immediately saw that the chamber was much larger than either hers or Frankie's. Like her own, it had windows that looked out onto the back gardens, but from the other side of the castle. The brocade curtains were closely drawn, which was a matter of relief to Jessica. There was no chance that Louis or Michael, looking up at the house from the patio, might see four figures moving about the room and wonder what they were doing there. It struck Jessica that even from a distance it was unlikely the four of them would be taken for exterminators working on an ant infestation.

She surveyed the perimeter of the bedchamber. It also had a four-poster bed, a desk, a vanity, and a large wardrobe. The upholstery of the furniture and bed hangings and the wallpaper were of higher quality than that in her room. "This is rather grand, isn't it?"

Alice responded with pride in the castle, which was now owned by her family, evident in her voice and momentarily replacing the sleuthlike demeanor she had assumed up until that point. "That it is. This was originally the room for the *lady of the castle*, I'll have you know."

"Evelyn Lansing's room?" Jessica asked in astonishment, looking about the room again with even more interest.

"Why yes. My ma told me so a long time ago. That's the reason Frankie Alexis wanted this room. But after a while, she had to move to the new room—the one that she was found in—because Ma told her she was very sorry but Mr. Thornes had this specific room already booked for his arrival with Mr. Aspen."

The room that Michael Thornes was installed in appeared as neat as a pin. No clothes were thrown over chair backs or on the floor, although the bed was still unmade from the night before. There were no loose papers scattered about.

Alain and Jessica started methodically examining the room from the outer to the inner spaces of the chamber. Joel stood guard by the door to the corridor while his sister peeked through the slit in the curtains out to the patio to assure all remained copacetic. Alain and Jessica were extremely careful to put back anything that they disturbed from its carefully placed position. They even pulled out the drawers of the end tables and lifted up the mattress, but no notebooks were there. There were none on or in the desk or in the wardrobe, where Thornes's clothes were neatly hung. The bathroom was also clear. They also looked in the cabinet under the sink in desperation, but all to no avail.

"I guess I was wrong," Jessica finally said, looking at the three other faces around her. "I feel like I should hang my head in shame. Joel and Alice, I'm sorry that I put you to all this trouble and risked your mother's anger by breaking and entering another guest's room." She bit her lip in frustration, nearly drawing blood.

"Wait a minute. Not so fast," Alice suddenly blurted out. Then she covered her mouth with her hand, as though recalling that she was supposed to whisper. "I remember now something Ma also told me."

Alice walked purposely over to the wall next to the desk. She pushed in hard on the paneling, just below where it met the wallpaper above it. The sound of a hinge releasing its clasp could be heard. And the paneling came back slightly toward her so that there was a small gap between its edge and that of the paneling to the side. Alice curled her fingers around the edge closer to her and pulled it back to reveal a small recess that had been previously unapparent.

She leaned over the darkened interior space, just as before Brenda had leaned over the safe. But Alice was more successful than her mother had been. She reached inside the dark space and pulled out a few well-worn notebooks from deep inside. The covers of the notebooks had picked up some of the old dust from the space behind the paneling. She brushed off a few of the flakes and waved the notebooks triumphantly over her head.

Then she asked, "Are these what you're looking for?"

Nineteen
The Notebooks

[Evelyn Lansing's notebooks with notations by Frankie Alexis.]
These notebooks, dear reader, hold all my thoughts and hopes and stories that spring from and fill my heart. I have been told by my husband, Bailey, that to publish them would not be "fitting" to my station in life, which must be so very exalted that my mere writings would put it at risk. Oh, but I would eagerly risk my station except for being so restrained. I have been instructed to relegate my writings to these little notebooks that only I can see. But I have the perverse hope that someday you, dear reader, will see them as well. And by that happy event I will defy, in a sense, my instructions by addressing all my words to you.

Jessica read Evelyn's introduction slowly and out loud to Alain. All the original entries had been written in a tidy, little script. And clipped to them were numerous handwritten notes by Frankie. Frankie's handwriting was bolder, almost erratic. It was as if her hand could not keep up the hectic pace of transcribing the many thoughts flowing from her active brain as she read what Evelyn had written. Additional notes, written in a different handwriting from the other two, were clipped to Frankie's clippings. Jessica and Alain, with Joel and Alice's help, had rapidly photocopied as many of the pages of each of the three notebooks and their annotations as they could before Lora's warning heralded that they were nearly out of time and that Thornes was returning to his room.

Jessica and Alain were sequestered in Jessica's bedchamber, in the opposite wing of the castle to where the notebooks had been discovered. Joel and Alice had assured them they wouldn't be disturbed by any staff member so that they could survey in private the notebook copies for any possible clues. The photocopied pages were scattered all over the bed, with spillage on the floor on either side of it. The bedchamber looked as if a window had been inadvertently left open and the pages scattered in every possible direction. But there was an order to the pages lying around, despite their haphazard appearance. Jessica had organized first the stories and then the commentaries written by the two other contributors. One had clearly been Frankie Alexis, who sadly was now deceased, as was the woman she had been studying: Evelyn Lansing.

"Sad, isn't it, that Evelyn was stuck in a situation with which she was obviously so unhappy?" Jessica said. "I mean, not to be able to use her good mind to its fullest potential and give it a voice for anyone around her to hear. But she must have believed that someday someone would eventually listen to her, or she wouldn't have written as she did and put so much of herself into her writings. Look at the stories she's written. They're quite lively and adventurous for someone so constrained by social expectations of what her place in the world should be."

The notebooks, though small, had been chock-full of tales. Jessica and Alain had only had time to photocopy a small sampling of them.

"I understand your feelings, but I'm more concerned that we still don't know if anything that Evelyn Lansing wrote all those years ago is associated with what led to Frankie Alexis's death," Alain said. "It's still only speculation on our part. I'm much more interested in what Frankie Alexis, and possibly Thornes, might have written about them. What either of *those two* wrote is more pertinent to the problem at hand."

Jessica nodded in agreement and placed the photocopied sheets of Evelyn Lansing's writings to the side of the bed. Then she took those of Frankie's pages and those of the additional ones that had been clipped to them. She and Alain both scanned them.

"Frankie's pages are cogent analyses of Evelyn Lansing's stories; they're detailed notes and seem to discuss the psychosexual meanings that Frankie drew from what she had read," Jessica said.

"She must have been branching out from crime fiction," Alain said.

"Yes, it looks like she may have decided to start writing nonfiction, doesn't it? Maybe she was going to use them as the backbone of a book of her analyses?"

"Possibly. If we consider what Alice told us, Frankie must have found the hidden compartment with the notebooks in Evelyn's old room and started on her own project. When Thornes got the room from her, if these are indeed his notes, as we think they are, he must have as well. Although it doesn't make sense that Frankie would have left them in her original room. So alternatively, and probably much more likely, Frankie shared her secrets with Thornes, for one reason or another."

"And Frankie ended up dead because of them," Jessica said grimly.

"We still don't know that. What we've seen so far doesn't seem significant enough to me to lead to murder. Let's take a look at what else was written down."

Jessica lifted up the last few sheets they had copied with the notes discussing Frankie's notations on the original stories of Evelyn Lansing. There were only a few of the third-party notes. They both scanned the pages together. "Why, it looks like it's jottings for consideration of a screenplay or a documentary," Jessica said. "I guess we weren't the only items on their list! I wonder if we should be insulted!"

"Seems he wasn't sure which one he wanted to start working on," Alain added. "In any case, I think it's finally time we spoke to Thornes—and Aspen—and not about *our* project."

****

Jessica and Alain found Thornes and Aspen with Brenda's assistance, but the woman cast a suspicious eye when asked where the two men might be. Jessica wondered if Alice was indeed correct: maybe Brenda did have "ears everywhere." But Brenda said nothing except that the pair was again conferring in the castle's library.

When Jessica and Alain entered the library, no martinis were on display; only a large pot of coffee and two cups and saucers sat on a tray between the two men.

Aspen immediately asked, "So what's the final decision?"

Alain sat down next to Jessica, who had deposited herself on the sofa, across from the other two. He said, "Unfortunately, that decision is still on hold, and it's likely to remain so for the near future."

Michael picked up his coffee cup, rattling it in its saucer so vigorously that he spilled some of the hot liquid onto the table. He took a clean linen napkin from the coffee tray and wiped up the spillage, seemingly engrossed in his task. Whatever was crossing his mind was obscured by his bowed head while he focused on this activity. But if something had bothered him, it appeared to fly right over his partner's head; Louis Aspen showed absolutely no loss of his usual air of self-confidence. The producer flashed a bright, toothsome smile at Alain and merely asked, "Oh, why so?"

Jessica wondered if Thornes had realized that the notebooks in his possession had been disturbed from their hiding place. He seemed so ill at ease. She unconsciously bit her lip, causing it to bleed, as she struggled to remember if they had replaced the three notebooks exactly as they had found them. Maybe the removal of some of the dust from their covers had been the problem? She just couldn't remember exactly. But she didn't have much time to contemplate that possibility; she needed to listen to what Alain was saying.

"It looks as though the recent death of Frankie Alexis has raised some difficult issues," Alain said.

"In what way?" Louis asked, raising his eyebrows. "I really can't imagine why that should affect *your* decision as to *your* project. People have a very short attention span for these kinds of things. Believe me. I know. It's the nature of the beast. Who can tell? But it might even be helpful to the project. Do forgive me for putting it somewhat coarsely." Louis reached over, picked up a cup, leisurely took a sip of coffee, and put the cup down again.

Alain ignored the gesture and said, "Let me explain then. For one thing, there's the matter of Frankie's writings, of which she was so possessive. If we ignore the unlikely possibility that the ghost of Evelyn Lansing has come back from the grave and is behind all this, Evelyn's notebooks, Frankie's annotations regarding their contents, and your own written thoughts on those of those two women, Michael, were all discovered hidden in your room. That makes for quite an interesting scenario. Almost a good plot for a new project. Don't you think, eh?"

Michael finally stopped sopping up the coffee spill and threw down the napkin in anger. "I told you, Louis, those notebooks were in a different spot from where I left them. And you said I was imagining it!"

"Oh, do be quiet, Michael! OK, it's obvious you've found the notebooks. Big deal! Michael here—with all of his dramatic instincts—obviously left them in the *perfect* spot for a script but the *dumbest* spot not to be found. But no matter. We might as well explain. We're not as ghoulish as you seem to imagine. You see, Frankie was not as successful as she liked to put on. Unconsciously, perhaps, but in any case, she was living a lie. But eventually, 'reality'"—[he paraphrased the word with two fingers of each hand]—"'reared its ugly head.' She needed cash, and she needed it bad. She had been researching the life of Evelyn Lansing. It was a type of obsession for her. But she was doing it on her own dime. That's why she was so eager for cash. Anyway, in the course of her work, she came upon the woman's undiscovered writings. And she hoped they might have monetary value. But they turned out not to be worth what she thought they would be. She apparently showed them to the local antiques dealer, who burst her balloon, and she was devastated."

"Are you talking about Paul Callahan?" Jessica asked.

"Yes. I think that was his name. He advised her to donate them to a local historical society or some such thing. Anyway, she came to us instead. And Michael here thought they'd make the basis for some stories that we could probably tie into your project. We told her she could still work on her own biography of Evelyn Lansing if she wanted to. We really didn't care about that. Anyway, we came up with the idea for her to dress up like Evelyn Lansing for the party to cause some publicity buzz that might be helpful down the road. That's why she was dressed in that ridiculous way that night. But *that's all* we discussed."

"Is that true?" Jessica asked.

"Yes! I'm telling you the truth. The reason we have her notebooks is that, before she dressed up that night, she gave them to Michael to see what she came up with so far. And when she was found dead, Michael and I thought it better to keep them under wraps. We didn't want to get further involved; it might adversely affect our future projects if it came out that we had a connection to her. But what I've told you is all our involvement was. Neither of us had anything to do with whatever followed her dressing up that night. If there's one thing that I've learned from past experience, it's not to push temperamental artists past their breaking points. Nobody wins if you do."

Jessica knew immediately that Louis was thinking back to his past experience with Beatrice Jones. Her guess was confirmed by his very next statement.

"An actress I used to know ended up leaving me for just such a mistake. And being familiar with both of your true detective skills—and I include you, Jessica, in that description, giving credit where it's due—I'm sure you've already become acquainted with my former muse, Beatrice."

Neither Jessica nor Alain bothered to hedge on that point. There was no need to. Louis Aspen was moving on in his monologue.

"Anyway, neither I nor Michael has any idea what might have driven Frankie to push the buzz further than we discussed, or even if she was working with any other party that we're not aware of. So I apologize, but I believe the two of you are at a *dead end*, sort to speak."

Twenty
The Doctor Makes
a House Call

Jessica and Alain left the library but were soon cornered by Brenda Ryan in the main hall of the castle. The woman was panting deeply as she leaned over to catch her breath before saying, "I'm so glad I found you both. I just got a call from Dr. Matthews. He asked if you would meet him at his office right away. He's there now. He opened it up and will wait until you come. He didn't tell me what it's about but he made it sound urgent. I told Alvin to have the car ready for you both."

"Fine," Alain said. "Please tell the doctor we'll come over there now."

"That I'll do!" She turned away from them and quickly limped over to the reception desk to relay Alain's message to Dev Matthews.

Jessica and Alain left the castle and walked over to the gardening shed. True to Brenda's word, they found the car waiting for them as promised, with the keys left inside on the dashboard. The gardener was nowhere to be found.

"Are you up for driving on the left side of the road?" Jessica asked. "I'm getting the feeling you're ready for the challenge."

"I think I can manage." He opened the passenger door for her and gestured for her to hop in. He walked around to the driver's side on the right, got in, and started the engine, which turned over after a few false starts.

They drove back toward the center of town as Jessica, now more confident of her surroundings, directed Alain to make the correct turn off to the road with Dev Matthews's medical office. On the way, Jessica barely noticed the flora around her; no longer did she relish the bright-yellow color of the low-lying gorse or the deep-green shading of the hedgerows surrounding her. She was much too focused on what reason the doctor might have for asking them to meet him. The urgency that Brenda had displayed earlier was acutely transmitted to Jessica, and she was finding it difficult to control her impatience until they reached their destination. It could only be that Matthews had more information to impart regarding Frankie's untimely death. She could think of no other reason for the hurried summons.

Finally, they reached Matthews's office, and Jessica breathed a sigh of relief. They parked out in front and went inside. As before, the office was totally quiet, this time more expectedly as it was a Sunday. Soon, Matthews came out from his consultation room and ushered them both into it. He took his seat behind his desk, facing them.

"Thank you both for coming so quickly. I wanted to talk to you because I just received a call from the detectives who are working the case of Frankie Alexis's death. I think you are already aware of them: detectives Byrne and Smith. They're both good men. I've had some interactions with them in the past. They do their jobs well but also have some imagination. Now I don't want to keep you both on tenterhooks, so I'll be brief. They arranged for some further analyses and were able to specifically identify the substance that led to Frankie Alexis's death."

"What did the analysis show?" Jessica asked.

"It showed what none of us knew before—that the chemical composition of the sample of what Frankie must have drank was identical to the recipe that I have used to compound Amy Stanwich's sleeping medications. I've been making them up for her for a long time. Amy's a doughty old woman, but she has depended on them for many years—without any problems, I might add. She's in excellent health for her age. It's quite re-markable, really."

"Do you think someone got a hold of your mixture?" Alain asked.

"No. Not at all. I make it fresh for Amy each time. And I don't leave any extra around the office. Even if my cabinets are locked, I like to be careful about things like that. And none of the ingredients I use are missing from my cabinets. That's what I came here to double-check. I did that before I called Brenda and asked her to find you and have you come over to meet me."

"Maybe someone got it from Amy?" Jessica suggested.

"I thought of that, but I dole out so little to Amy at a time. I can't imagine someone would get enough from her, without her knowing, to be able to hurt anyone in any way. But I can't otherwise explain the match that Byrne and Smith found. Look, I didn't talk to Amy yet. I didn't want to distress someone of her age, even with her overall good health. So I thought I'd first run the scenario by you both and see what you think—you, Inspector Raynaud, with your expertise, and you, Jessica—Dr. Shepard, I should say—with your experience. I wanted to get a second opinion, in a matter of speaking, and from two with a little distance from the local community."

"What did the detectives say about this?" Alain asked.

"They want me to speak to Amy before they do. She's an old lady, and they want to avoid frightening her if they don't need to. She lives alone, you must know, in that cottage. It's somewhat isolated there. And if she thought anyone did get into her home and took some of her *medicine,* I don't know what would happen. I mentioned that to the detectives and asked for some time. I told them I'd discuss it with you and I'd ask you to help me break the news to Amy and see what she has to say. I've explained to you, Jessica, it's a small town. People know and care about each other here." He looked at them from across his desk with such an earnest expression that Jessica found it hard to resist.

She turned to Alain and said, "I think the doctor makes a good point. Can you stay a little longer, Alain, so we have time to help him out with this?"

Alain smiled. "Don't worry. When I got your call in the first place, I made arrangements, just in case my *weekend* might need to be extended. I've learned from past experience that with you one thing usually leads to another."

****

Amy Stanwich's cottage appeared exactly as Jessica remembered, and as Matthews had remarked, it was isolated. Jessica, Alain, and the doctor approached it, and as before, Amy's little dog began to bark, even before they had time to ring the bell. They could hear the animal being shushed away from the door and into another part of the house. Then, a few minutes later, Amy opened the door.

She was attired in the same suit she was wearing when Jessica first met her on the patio of Castle Ryan. Again, the watch and fob, that throwback to an earlier age, hung from the woman's jacket lapel. Amy glanced quickly at it, as though to firmly impress upon her mind the time of the unexpected arrival of her visitors.

"Amy, my dear, may we come in?" Dev Matthews asked his patient and old friend.

"Of course, Dev. Yes, do. I was just going to make myself a nice cup of hot tea. Please, all of you, come in, and I'll make a fresh pot for all of us." She moved back from the door.

As this was the first time Jessica gained entry to the interior of the cottage, she was very interested in seeing it with her own eyes. She had only glanced at it through the window on her prior foray. The cottage was tidy. The entry hall had a multi-color, shag rug on the floor, and there was a parlor to one side of the hall to welcome guests, who were unlikely to be many. A small dining room was opposite the parlor on the other side of the hall. The dining table looked as though it was frequently rubbed with a good quantity of beeswax to reach the high level of shine on its top. But otherwise, the tableau of the empty room, with its knickknacks and dishes stored neatly away in glass cabinets, was one of protected disuse.

Amy led her party of three into the parlor, where two small sofas were positioned across from each other on either side of the large fireplace, which was currently unlit. Still, the room felt stiflingly hot. Jessica looked around, disappointed to see that none of the windows in the room were open; there would be no refreshing breeze of country air coming in from the outside.

In the corner of the room was a side chair with a lace antimacassar hung over its back. It supported a Victorian doll that sat primly; the doll's porcelain face and dark, painted eyes stared out blankly at them, as though bemused to find three guests had finally been invited into the parlor.

On the mantelpiece were a few black-and-white photographs of Amy's dog and the gardens behind Castle Ryan. Jessica immediately recognized the gardens in the photos as those she had walked through at the castle, and she went over to better inspect them.

Amy noticed Jessica looking at the photos and said, "Yes, Jessica, those are prints of the gardens that I sold to the Ryans. But I couldn't sell my photos of the gardens. No, those, *at least*, I kept. I had them commissioned for me when I was much younger. It gives me so much pleasure to stare at them on a rainy day. Aren't the gardens beautiful, even when reproduced in photographic form?"

"They certainly are," Jessica agreed.

"Alvin Hill used to work for me, you know. But he went with the land, sort to speak. That was *one* condition of the sale on which I wouldn't budge. Of course, now he must answer to a new mistress. But he keeps the grounds as pretty as they used to be, I'm happy to say. I like to keep an eye on them when I lunch there. They're still like my old friends."

"I can imagine," Jessica added.

"Yes, well, no matter. I must stop being such a discursive, old woman. Why don't we all sit down, and I'll get the tea for us to drink? You like it strong, if I remember correctly, Dev. Isn't that right?"

"Yes, I do, Amy, but—" Dev said gently.

"Jessica, do sit down, dear. You can sit down with your handsome, gentleman friend on one of the sofas, and when I come back with the tea, I can sit with Dev on the other."

Jessica took a seat with Alain next to her.

"Why Jessica, what a pretty, little bracelet! It looks familiar to something I used to wear when I was younger." Jessica suddenly had the awful sensation that perhaps the bracelet she had been so pleased with was yet another of Amy's treasures that had made its way to the sale block and to Callahan's antiques shop.

"Amy, why don't we wait on the tea?" Matthews said.

"Oh, why? Have you already had yours, Dev?"

"Sit down, Amy, please." Matthews helped Amy to the empty sofa and sat down beside her, taking her hand in his. Both their hands, with signs of age in the creases of skin, were now enfolded in each other. Jessica and Alain were sitting opposite to them, as Amy had requested. Matthews nodded at Jessica, giving her leave to begin speaking to Amy as one woman to another.

"Amy, the reason we wanted to talk to you was that Dr. Matthews heard back from the police about Frankie Alexis."

"That was so sad, wasn't it?" Amy said.

Jessica continued. "It seems that the sleeping medicine that caused her to stop breathing was identical to the mixture the doctor compounded for you." Jessica allowed her words to seep into the older woman's consciousness.

Rather than confusion though, Jessica could perceive immediate comprehension in Amy's eyes; they seemed to brighten with a startling glint. Amy then leaned over to one side and turned on the small lamp on the end table beside her; it was as though the gesture mirrored the breakthrough of the woman's brain as it focused sharply on what Jessica was saying.

"Go on," Amy directed after the light had been turned on.

"We wondered where you might have stored what the doctor gave you and if it was possible that anyone else could have gotten a hold of it before it made its way to Frankie."

"I see." Amy looked around her at the perimeter of her tidy parlor. And then she said, "Well, no. No one else would have been able to get it. You see, I do not employ servants any longer. I have no need for them now. But I certainly don't mind showing you all where I keep the concoctions that my old friend, Dev, has so kindly given me over the years."

She gently extracted the one hand that had still remained in Matthews's gentle hold. "Just let me go upstairs first and straighten up my bedchamber. You see, I still consider myself a lady. And in my day, we were taught to have our bedchambers in perfect order before anyone was allowed into them."

Amy got up and left the room.

"Well, that went better than expected," Jessica said once she, Dev, and Alain were alone.

"I'm not so sure," Matthews said uncertainly. "I've known her for so many years, and she took the suggestion about the match of the sleeping medicines too easily. As I said, she's a doughty old woman, and I've never seen her to act so placidly, at least that I can remember. She should have at least challenged your theory with some probing—and confrontational—questions."

He hesitated a few moments and then said, "If she doesn't come down in a minute or two, I'm going up there and see what's going on."

"Better not wait," Alain said. "Go up now."

Matthews rose up from his seat. With an agility that belied his age and must have come from years of making so many visits to so many homes around the Irish town, he left the parlor and rapidly climbed the stairs to the second floor. Jessica heard the thumping of his steps on the stairs and then the sound moved into a room overhead of the parlor. Suddenly, they heard Matthews call out shrilly, "Amy! Amy!"

In a flash, Alain was up and out of the room, with Jessica only a step behind him. They flew up the stairs, following Matthews's anguished cries as guidance. Alain took the narrow steps two at a time, his long legs easily managing the feat while Jessica did her best to keep up. On the upper landing, a door to one of the rooms was wide open and they both ran up to it.

Around Alain's broad back, Jessica was able to see Matthews leaning over the recumbent form of Amy Stanwich. The old woman was lying full length on the bed, her toes curled to either side of her and one fist clutching the bedding. She must have taken off her shoes before lying down on the coverlet; the pair of shoes had been neatly arranged on the side of the bed, the tips pointing outward to the door. The way the toes were angled made Jessica momentarily think back to what Frankie's own feet had looked like when the woman's dead body was sprawled on the floor of the bedchamber at Castle Ryan.

But Jessica had to focus back on this new body: silvery froth was coming out of Amy's mouth and dripping down from one corner to the top of the elderly woman's chin. And Amy's little dog was barking hysterically on the far side of the room, the saliva exiting his mouth almost matching in quantity the liquid smearing the cold lips of his mistress.

"She's taken an overdose!" Matthews shouted, sensing their entry into the room and turning around and away from his patient for just a quick moment. "There was a letter in her hand. I don't have time to read it now. Jessica, go down into the kitchen. Her phone's in there. *Call an ambulance.*" He barked out the number Jessica was to call.

Jessica hurried back down the stairs and into the kitchen, which was as tidy as the parlor had been. She took no time to take in its contents except to locate the phone attached to the far wall by the sink. She dialed the number Matthews had given her, surprised that her hands weren't shaking, and once she was sure help was on the way, she ran back up the stairs.

"They're coming." The words spilled out of her mouth, despite the breathlessness she felt from running up and down the stairs and the feverish beating of her heart.

"Good. Take this letter." Matthews pushed it into Jessica's outstretched hand. "We'll look at it later. Alain, Help me. I need to get her up. She must have been saving them. I think she took enough to kill her. I have nothing with me to pump out her stomach."

The two men fumbled with Amy's unresponsive form.

What seemed like an agonizingly long time later, they then heard the sound of an ambulance crunching the gravel in the driveway as it came to a rapid halt in front of the cottage. Jessica ran back down the stairs, pushing the letter that Matthews had given her into her pocket. She pulled open the front door to let in the medics. They followed her up the stairs, and soon they brought Amy down on a stretcher and out to the waiting ambulance. Matthews, Jessica, and Alain were close behind and watched as the back doors of the van swallowed up the stretcher.

"I'm going to hospital with them!" Mathews shouted at Jessica and Alain from the doors of the van. Then he got into the van, settling his older body down next to the stretcher on which Amy was lying. As Jessica watched him do that, it suddenly seemed as if the knowledge of his advanced age had returned to the doctor once his patient was out of the cottage and in the ambulance. His back was curled forward over Amy's body. He left Jessica and Alain behind as the gravel dust blew up in their faces, caused by the retreating flight of the van rushing away from Amy's tidy home.

Twenty-one
The Letter

To my dear friend, Dr. Dev Matthews,

I write this letter in case what I have done is found out. I would not want anyone to cast blame on you, old friend. As you are now reading it, I must assume discovery has occurred.

Let me start by reminding you of my history, which may make my actions more understandable. I wouldn't dare to write "forgivable." I was born and have lived all my many years in this town that I call my home. I have remained by myself most of my life. But I have not been alone. My best friends—outside of my little dogs, who have entered and left my company over time, and you, of course—have been my cottage and the land surrounding it.

But time passes, and money needs become a new "acquaintance" to which attention must be paid, no matter how distasteful. So as you are aware, I was finally forced to relinquish by sale some of those precious acres, of which I have known every inch since childhood. What else could I do? I sold them to Bevin Ryan and his family for his Castle Ryan. And try as I might by drinking tea and eating pastries on their patio among the flowers and visiting those acres like the old friends they were, in truth, I knew they were no longer mine. Their loss pulled more and more at my heart until it was like a virulent cancer growing ever stronger inside me.

Serendipitously—you will probably think that an ironic choice of words—I learned from Frankie Alexis of her plan to create publicity for her writings about Evelyn Lansing and of a television series that might be filmed on my cherished land. You see, I still describe it as "my." But not to digress, I learned of her conversation with a producer and a screenwriter. No one really pays attention to my presence anymore. I am just an old woman past her prime. So who cares if I hear such blasphemy?

To open up those cherished acres to packs of people filming a television series, I couldn't allow that, now could I? And what if floods of tourists arrived to trample my cherished gardens if the series were successful? I knew that Brenda and Bevin Ryan wouldn't resist the chance for such profits as I would have. They would have been complicit in the destruction. I was so angry when I heard this that I had to do something drastic to stop Frankie from appearing that night dressed like Evelyn Lansing and causing a hullabaloo about the castle's history. And I did.

You see, Dev, I have never needed as much help to sleep as I put on. Most of my recent requests for your visits were just to pass the too long hours of the day, which you probably guessed. But you were too kind to let me know that you knew my reason for most of those visits. So I saved your medicine, but bit by bit. And I found I had accumulated quite a little store. I carried them around to have available if I ever got the courage to use them. You see, I had originally thought to use them for myself. But then when I heard what was being contemplated, I thought of an even better idea.

So the night of the gala, I gave them to Frankie. She was nervous about her publicity plan to dress up like the long-departed Evelyn Lansing; she wanted to continue to raise the specter of Evelyn's ghostly reappearance for the reasons I already alluded to, but she was getting cold feet. She was starting to feel it was beneath her. She did have her standards. But unfortunately, such was my anger that I misjudged the dose and gave Frankie so much that it was she who was no more. I must also confess that I have come to feel that if she had to die, and it caused fewer visitors to Castle Ryan and to "my" cherished gardens, I would at least derive some sense of retribution for my loss of them by sale.

And when or if I am found out, not being brave enough to confess these thoughts verbally, I will have already written this confession to safeguard you. And then I will take my leave in peace.

Amy Stanwich

****

Jessica finished reading the letter aloud to Matthews, Alain, and detectives Byrne and Smith, and then she handed it over to the two detectives. The five of them were at the hospital where Amy had been taken. But she had not pulled through. The hospital was a distance from Amy's cottage, and the doctors there hadn't been able to revive the old woman who had gotten the wish she had expressed in her last letter to Dev Matthews.

"I guess that settles it," Detective Byrne said. He was one of the two detectives Dev Matthews had described earlier as having "some imagination." It had been his insistence on additional analysis of the chemical composition of the means of Frankie Alexis's death that had tied it to Amy's possession and led to the confrontation before the elderly woman took her own life.

Had Amy's letter displayed any sense of contrition for the act she had performed that had ended Frankie's life, intentionally or unintentionally? Jessica wasn't sure. Jessica had closely read the letter, paying special attention to Amy's use of the term "retribution." Jessica's analysis made her feel that the letter was more a confessional about the thoughts Amy had had rather than what Amy had done. But at least it seemed that Amy had shown enough loyalty and gratitude to Dev Matthews, who had unselfishly cared for her for so long, that she had wanted to spare the generalist from any associated blame for what had transpired at her hands.

All these thoughts that were running through Jessica's mind seemed to be lost on Detective Byrne, who despite his "imagination" appeared satisfied at the closure of his latest case. The detective had discovered Frankie Alexis's cause of death and the connection between the means of her demise to substances owned and provided by the perpetrator, who was now conveniently deceased, and justice had been served. Jessica understood that the detective was similarly pleased that the letter Jessica had just read to him exonerated the local physician; it was another complication he wouldn't be forced to deal with.

She wondered if the other detective, Smith, felt the same way. That question was answered for her when Detective Smith concurred with his partner with a brief vertical nod of his head. They were almost like twins, Jessica thought. Detective Byrne had afforded himself the custodian of Amy's letter. He folded it carefully and placed it in his breast pocket. Then both men left the other three without any further conversation.

"I still can't believe it," Matthews said, shaking his head slowly back and forth, as though the motion would illuminate for him a better understanding of the elderly woman who had consulted the generalist for so many years. "I have always prided myself on understanding my patients. But at least in this case, I missed so much. *So much.* And mind you, I knew that Amy had her quiddities. I'll grant you that. But I never figured her capable of doing what she did—not for one minute. And now she's finally gone. I can't believe it."

Jessica could see that Dev was wracked with guilt. No degree of exoneration was provided him by Amy's letter, no matter how detailed the elderly woman's explanation had been. Jessica remembered all the interactions she had witnessed between the two: that first night at the ball when Matthews had so gallantly escorted Jessica and Amy into dinner; his control of the horrific situation when Frankie's body had been discovered and the way he had insisted Amy get rest after that night; and finally, the gentle confrontation with Amy in the privacy of her cottage and his valiant attempt to save the woman's life, no matter what she had done—all without success.

Jessica knew that it was now her turn to provide comfort to the elder physician. Byrne and Smith were gone, eager to be on their way to whatever new case they would need to solve. And Alain, no matter how Jessica had come to know that the inspector had a gentler side under his tough outer skin, also was not the appropriate one to do it. So she moved over to sit by Matthews and talk to him.

"You can't blame yourself," Jessica said, placing her hand on the other physician's arm in comfort. "None of us truly understood what demons were inside her. If we had, we still probably wouldn't have been able to guess Amy would have done what she did. And even Frankie herself, who seemed so strong and independent, obviously couldn't fathom what Amy would do—or Frankie never would have so readily accepted anything from Amy's hand!"

"Well, I still can't help believing that if I were the type of physician that I always prided myself as being, I wouldn't have failed to see this all coming, or at least I would have put it together sooner than I did. I don't know. I think it's time for me to start thinking about taking down my shingle at last. But before I do, I have to talk to the Ryans, especially Brenda. She's also my patient, you know."

Jessica had no doubt that no matter what words were springing forth from Matthews in the heat of despair and tiredness, it would be many years before this town would lose the services of its physician if he had anything to do about it. Matthews got up from his chair, removing Jessica's hand from his arm and patting it gently. It ran through her mind that it was a similar gesture to the one she had seen him make to Amy at her cottage the last night of Amy's life. Jessica pushed that thought from her mind and let it settle far from her. Instead, she smiled at Dev to give him further encouragement that things would improve for him with time. It seemed to help.

Fatigue was clearly evident in the slow but determined motion of his body as he hoisted himself onto his feet. Once standing, he seemed to regain some vim and vigor. He looked at Jessica and at Alain, who had remained silent since the other detectives had left the hospital. Jessica knew that Alain had allowed her to handle the generalist's insecurities without interruption. And for that she was grateful.

Dev asked, "Will you both drop me at my office? I want to call Brenda. And I want to throw out my compounding equipment. I'll not be doing any more of that, at the very least! If I'm asked, I'll refer them to Dublin!"

Twenty-two
Back to the Castle

Jessica and Alain dropped off Matthews at his office and headed back to Castle Ryan. Alain drove, now fairly confident in the right-sided driver's seat. Jessica laughed to herself, recalling how that little bit of unfamiliarity had at first unsettled her, and then Alain, considering all that had transpired since then. That recollection was a light moment in an otherwise glum finish to the last few days; they would somehow need to break the spell. Perhaps Alain would be able to further extend his time with her, hopefully not to handle any more murder cases—at least not for the near future.

Neither spoke as the car rambled along the narrow lane back up the hill to the castle. The events of the last few hours were too disturbing for conversation. Each was cocooned in their own thoughts about how everything had panned out. Several minutes passed, and then they reached the castle, which stood silently in the expanse of greenery surrounding it. Nothing about the castle's appearance suggested it had been the nidus for so much drama, recently and in the past; to Jessica it looked the same, despite all that had occurred. And she couldn't fail to recall her arrival that first day with only thoughts of whether or not to consider a television project revolving around her and Alain's recent experiences.

Jessica suddenly wondered how Sean and Millie were doing and if they had already learned of all that had happened at Castle Ryan. Jessica also remembered Millie's Grandmother Rose. She could envision Rose and her nurse, Martha Robson, sitting together in that big, old-fashioned kitchen in Killiney, drinking tea and exclaiming over Amy Stanwich's demise. That would be a story for Rose to retell. But Jessica knew it would not be one that the nonagenarian would take any pleasure in. But what of the McLeish sisters, Iris and June, the tall one and the short one? Would they relate the details again and again over their tea in Millie's coffee shop?

As the car lurched over the gravel drive, Jessica's tumultuous thoughts finally settled down into place. They drove around the side of the castle and soon pulled up to the gardening shed in the back. Alain turned off the car's engine, and Jessica looked up to see Alvin Hill come out from the interior of the shed.

The gardener looked like he had the first time Jessica met him. He was still wearing the high gardening boots that always were part of his standard garb. But this time, the boots were wiped totally clean. It struck Jessica that the news of Amy's death must have lent enough solemnity that, even for a gruff man like Alvin Hill, some higher level of respect was thought appropriate; after all, Amy's demise was the sad finale of a long life he must have witnessed in happier days. Alvin cast a subdued smile in their direction as a type of greeting, which Jessica caught through the car window.

"Working on a Sunday?" Jessica asked as she and Alain exited the car.

"I heard about Miss Stanwich," Alvin said. He looked down at those clean boots as though studying them for any flaws and then said, "Sad day it is all around. I've known her for so many years. She changed so but I still can't believe what I heard." He paused again before saying, "Amy was quite a looker when she was young. Oh, you wouldn't know it now. But in her youth, all the young lads wanted her to give them the time of day."

"Is that right?" Jessica asked.

"Yes. But she wouldn't have much to do with any of them. All she wanted to do was care for her father until his very last days. You see, she lost her mother when she was young. So she sort of considered it her charge to do so. And of course, she loved her gardens. So I always did my best to keep them as beautiful as I could for her, even when she had to sell them to the Ryans. But I can't believe she was responsible for the loss of another life, especially as she loved her living garden so. Just doesn't make sense."

Alvin still looked down thoughtfully at his unusually clean boots. "Someone's got to take care of her little dog though. I think I'll talk to Dr. Matthews and see if it'll be all right if I take the little cur in. I can make a fine place for him in the shed."

He shook his head as he accepted the car keys from Alain. And Alvin walked back into the gardening shed, presumably to start working on Amy's little dog's new quarters.

News obviously had traveled fast. It seemed to Jessica that Alvin's reaction to the reports of Amy's actions and subsequent demise was so similar to that of Dr. Matthews. It reinforced her inherent belief that there is so little that one ever knows about any other person; she had misunderstood the gardener, as she had Amy. Alvin would have been the last person she would have thought would have been worried about a little dog. This latest episode was yet one more example of what was becoming her creed: that the human heart is a mystery and no matter how much you think you understand it, it always surprises you.

Jessica and Alain left the area by the shed and walked slowly back to the castle. They opened the heavy entrance door and went inside. The hall was quiet. Once again, Jessica looked up to see the massive chandelier sparkling overhead in the middle of the hall. Standing farther in, by the chairs that Alain and Jessica had used to plan their contributions to the solution of this latest case, and by the display case with Castle Ryan's coat of arms, stood the Ryans. The entire Ryan clan was assembled by the display case. They were staring at it as though wondering how all these recent events would reflect upon the shiny metal of the coat of arms. It was a rare situation where all four family members were gathered together at the same time. The last time Jessica remembered it so was the night Frankie Alexis had expired.

Bevin, head of his family, approached them and shepherded Jessica and Alain over to the other members of his family.

"We're glad you both are back," Bevin said. "We have so many questions. May we all talk in the library?"

Bevin led them inside the room that had hosted so many discussions over the past few days. Jessica and Alain positioned themselves on seating across from Bevin and Brenda. The fireplace wasn't lit that time of day, and it felt a little cold as it does when the last days of summer seem to allow a breeze to add some chill to the air. Jessica wasn't exactly sure if that was the reason for the coldness she felt or the fact that this was one more interview with persons who needed to obtain closure by reviewing the recent events surrounding Castle Ryan.

The Ryan progeny, Alice and Joel, stood stiffly behind their parents. Alice had one hand resting on her mother's shoulder in support. Joel had both hands behind him, as if in attention, like a soldier awaiting an order from a commanding officer.

Alain reviewed for them, in his usual didactic style, the events that had occurred over the past few hours, filling in any details that hadn't yet made their way up to the castle and to its inhabitants.

"She seemed so pleased with the sale of her property and her release from its burdens," Bevin said. "It boggles my mind that she harbored such animus inside her. If she had just consulted us, we would have assured her that even if we decided to expand the possibilities available at Castle Ryan for other uses, we would always preserve the gardens. We love them almost as much as Amy does—*did*."

There it was, Jessica thought, one more set of people surprised by what Amy Stanwich had been capable of. But Jessica needed to give each his due. So she pushed the thought back from the front of her mind and continued to listen to what the Ryans had to say.

Brenda added, "Bevin, dear, we are just lucky, in a sense, that she didn't strike out at one of us. Although *poor* Miss Alexis. I'm still so *distraught* about that." She paused a moment to collect herself and then said, "Amy must have had such conflicted feelings toward us. She drank her tea here nearly every day! And to think what she was actually thinking! What was going through her mind!" Brenda shuddered visibly. Her daughter squeezed her shoulder, and the gesture seemed to soothe the older woman.

"Don't think about it anymore, love," Bevin directed. "It's over. Although there's one more thing I should mention. Do you know who turned out to be the silent, largest investor that Mr. Aspen was touching for his project?"

"No," Jessica said, looking at Alain to see if he had also failed to remember to think about that point.

"Why, Stanley Bogart!" Brenda blurted out. "It turns out he's very wealthy—*family money*." She mouthed the last two words. "Turned out that he wanted to help finance the project to help Frankie get enough money so she could continue to do all her writing that she loved so much. He just confessed this to me before you both got back from hospital. He had turned in some bonds and had the cash all ready. But he didn't want her to know about it. He didn't want her to think that he thought she couldn't succeed on her own and that she needed him. She was such an independent person!"

"What a shame!" Jessica said.

"Yes. He was devastated because he thought if he had only told her he had so much money, and what he planned to do with it, then she wouldn't have been so cash strapped and none of this would have happened. *Poor man.* The younger people now-adays—that's what's wrong with them. They never *talk* to each other, so they never know what each of them is thinking. It's all those cell phones and internet and all the other nonsense."

Brenda looked positively perplexed. Then she seemed to brighten up and said, "I'm sure he'll be staying on with us for a while to recover. We should move him to a bigger room, Bevin. Especially since Mr. Aspen and Mr. Thornes will be leaving. Although Mr. Aspen told me he has some new financing he's almost *got in the bag.*" This time she mouthed the last four words.

"Well, it is over," Jessica said for wont of anything else to say. Then she wrinkled her forehead in concentration. "By the way, are Mr. Aspen and Mr. Thornes still here, or have they left already?"

"Yes," Bevin said. "They'll be checking out. But they're still here now."

"Good," Jessica and Alain said with one voice.

Alain then added, "We have something to discuss with them."

Twenty-three
The Play's the Thing

Aspen and Thornes stood in the library with their luggage nestled at their feet. The four Ryans had left the room so that Jessica and Alain could talk privately with the television producer and the screenwriter. The two men appeared finally ready to decamp for good from the castle. As Brenda had rightly disclosed, now that Frankie Alexis was gone, and her literary career with her, Stanley Bogart had no further interest in Louis Aspen's project and the pianist would not be contributing financially to it.

But over the past half hour, Louis had tried valiantly to assure Jessica and Alain that he had every confidence in his ability to secure additional financing from other quarters; he was confident he would be able to make up the breach left by Bogart's exit from his proposed television series. Louis had also floated the option that perhaps either Jessica or Alain would be interested in providing some of their own funds to finance the project. As neither of them showed any interest in that, Louis had then confidently fallen back to his initial plan of obtaining other financing. And he had, only that instant, almost given up on his ability to convince either of them to go forward by just accepting that the recent events at Castle Ryan were only small bumps on the road to success.

But unable to avoid one last attempt to cajole Jessica and Alain, Aspen ended by saying, "Well, I guess your decision is final, but I think you're both making a big mistake." He was obviously not a man to easily give up even when all appeared to be going against his plans.

"Definitely final," Jessica said.

"Absolutely final," Alain said.

"I still think your stories would have made great television. But I guess it's *both your* losses and not *mine*." He turned to his partner who, although still next to him, was now halfway turned toward the wide-open door of the library as though the departure couldn't happen soon enough for him.

Jessica wondered if there would be some point, and what it would be, to finally dislodge Michael Thornes from the team of Aspen and Thornes. Jessica hoped it would not be as dramatic a point as the one that had finally caused the actress, Beatrice Jones, to have taken such leave. But at least for now, it appeared that Thornes was still waiting on his cue from Aspen before finally departing the scene.

"Michael, what do you say? Shall we head on out? Bigger and better projects to come!"

Then as though a new thought suddenly popped into his active brain, Louis once again directed his bright focus back to Jessica and Alain. "By the way, what are you two going to do now that we'll no longer be footing the bills for your stay here?" True curiosity was evident in his keen expression, and a deep furrow appeared between his eyebrows, crinkling them almost beyond recognition.

Jessica said quietly, "Oh. We've decided to head back to Dublin and spend some time there."

"Really? What do you plan to do?"

"I don't know. We might catch some plays—live theater and all that, you know."

Louis studied her closely, as if trying hard to determine if there might be a hidden meaning behind her seemingly innocuous words. But then he seemed to think better of it, as if he would be smart to leave some stones unturned. And he merely said, "Would have thought you had enough of that kind of thing here already."

"Yes. But this time, we want to be in the *audience* and not in the *cast*," Alain said firmly, practically ushering Aspen and Thornes out of the library door.

"Good idea. Good idea." Louis nodded his head up and down. And for once, finally, he appeared to have given up. Then he picked up his traveling bag, and before he joined Michael, who was now outside the library's door, he said, "Well, if you change your minds or work another case, just keep us in mind." He handed Jessica his business card and joined Michael outside of the room.

"Thanks. I'm sure we'll do that," Jessica called after him. And as the producer and the screenwriter left the castle, and she heard the heavy, oaken entrance door of Castle Ryan close behind the two men, Jessica placed Louis's card into Alain's hand and laughed. "Well, you never know!"

Twenty-four
All Ends Are Tied

"Now remember, Alain, Rose is ninety years old," Jessica said. "So don't overwhelm her."

"What makes you think I would do that?"

"I don't know. But just don't."

Jessica and Alain were driving up to Killiney. They were no longer in Castle Ryan's little, black car but were seated in a comfortable sedan that Alain insisted on renting. Jessica had been successful in coercing Alain to extend his stay in Ireland; her persuasive qualities had been particularly fruitful. The plan was to travel by car to Dublin for the sightseeing they had missed on their last foray to the city. But Alain's one condition had been only if they would do so in what he considered an acceptable car for the trip. And her conditions had been three preliminary stops before they could holiday. Jessica always needed to tie up loose ends. And this latest adventure was no exception to her rule.

Their first stop was at the home of Millie's grandmother Rose.

Alain stopped the car in front of the little house that Jessica had last visited with Millie. Millie had been only too gratified when Jessica had made known her intention to visit Rose before heading onward. Jessica got out of the car. In her hands was a portfolio of papers that she had quickly made up into a coffee-table book of sorts. She had found a local stationery store and, with the assistance of the proprietor, compiled the book as a gift to present to Rose. The gift was in gratitude for the old woman's hospitality. And it was also a way of expressing thanks for Rose's grand storytelling, which had first led Jessica on the trail of Evelyn Lansing's life story, even if that woman's tale had played a sad role in a modern-day tragedy.

Jessica rang the bell at the side of the front door. Martha, Rose's nurse, soon greeted them as she had greeted Jessica before.

"Jessica, come in," Martha said. "When Millie mentioned you would be stopping by, Rose could barely contain herself with anticipation for another visit."

"Thank you, Martha. This is my friend Alain. I brought him to see her as well."

Martha looked up at Alain appreciatively. "Oh, then she will be even happier. She still has an eye for a handsome gentleman." The nurse led Jessica and Alain back to Rose's kitchen, which seemed to be the chosen setting for all guests to the neat, little home.

Rose immediately appraised Jessica and Alain as they entered the kitchen. And once again, the old woman's intelligent, blue eyes sparked with delight at having new guests to entertain.

"Sit down, Jessica, and you, young man," Rose said.

"This is Alain," Martha explained. "Jessica brought him to also visit with you."

"Well then, sit down. Sit down."

Jessica and Alain pulled up two chairs to the large, wooden table and sat down. Jessica placed the book she had prepared on the table in front of her. It had a soft, leather cover of a brilliant blue. She had purposely chosen the color among the selections of leather in the stationery store. It matched the background of the sign over Callahan's antiques shop, the Gold Harp. The color of the leather and the color of the sign reminded Jessica of the hue of Rose's eyes and had seemed the perfect choice for the gift she was to present to the nonagenarian.

"What is this?" Rose asked.

Jessica leaned forward and opened up the large tome. Inside were photocopies of all the pages of the many stories that Evelyn Lansing had written all those years ago. Paul Callahan and Jessica had learned of and managed to locate by telephone the distant and only descendent of Evelyn Lansing. The descendent, who was currently living in Australia, assured of the lack of value of Evelyn Lansing's papers—and who was totally uninterested in them in any case—agreed that the pages could be copied and the originals could end up in a historical society's archives or anywhere else they saw fit. So Jessica had compiled the copies into a book for Rose to enjoy. The originals were now safely in Paul Callahan's possession for further disposition.

Jessica showed Rose the pages of stories. There were stories of garden fairies that frolicked in the woods around Castle Ryan, there were stories of hardship and the harvesting of the land, and there were stories of love in all its forms, requited and unrequited.

Rose turned the pages slowly and reverently and then said, "Thank you, Jessica. These will give me so much pleasure. They do remind me of my mother and of the stories she told me in my youth. They bring her back to life for me."

Martha chimed in. "Rose, don't forget that maybe now I can bring you down to your granddaughter's coffee shop, and you can read them for her patrons, like Millie suggested."

Rose laughed. "Now that's a thought, Martha. Maybe I'll do that. But for now, it's time to remember the dead and to celebrate the living. No tea today. Bring out the good whiskey. We have a lady and a gentleman with us!"

****

Jessica and Alain's next stop was back to Paul Callahan's antiques shop. Alain found a spot for the car close to the shop. They walked along the mercantile street until they came to the Gold Harp and entered. It looked exactly as it had the first time Jessica saw it; the clutter of cherished items for sale still provided enough ambiance to last a lifetime.

Jessica led Alain down the narrow aisle to the small room at the back of the store. But when she looked into it, she couldn't find Paul Callahan or Evelyn Lansing's portrait anywhere. "It's not there!" Jessica practically shouted as she pointed to the blank wall on which the painting had hung.

"Maybe it existed only in your imagination," Alain said.

"Don't be ridiculous," Jessica snapped, annoyed at his archness. "As Alvin Hill would likely say, 'I've not lost my marbles!' *It was there.* Look at the outline of the paint on the wall. You can see where it's darker around the edges and lighter in the interior where the portrait used to hang."

Just then Paul Callahan finally appeared from the back door at the far side of the little room.

"Why hello. How are you?" Callahan said. "By the way, I forgot to ask the last time I saw you, Jessica. Are you enjoying your bracelet?"

"Yes, I am. But I'm here now because I brought my friend, Alain Raynaud, to see Evelyn's portrait and I'm so disappointed to see that it's gone. I thought you said you would never sell it!"

"But, my dear, young lady, that is true. I haven't. Come back with me. I've just been getting it ready for transport. But I've only just begun, so you both can still catch a glance at it before it's all carted up."

"Is it going somewhere?" Jessica asked. "To a museum?"

"No. No. Come back here, and I'll tell you my exciting plan."

Callahan led Jessica and Alain into the second office. And there, stacked against a wall, was Evelyn's portrait, just like Callahan said. Jessica could see Alain's eyes appreciate the quality of the artwork as he ran his eyes over it. In the stronger light of the back room, the portrait was even more impressive than it had been in the space by Callahan's desk in the other room. After they all finished reviewing the beauty of the portrait, Callahan explained his plan as he had promised.

"Jessica, I know that you know details about Amy Stanwich's passing, so I'll not belabor you with Amy's backstory except to say that, of course, Amy had a will. And that document provided for me to purchase her cottage at a previously agreed-upon price in the event of her death, for whatever reason. I assure you this is all on the up-and-up. Well, I am, of course, planning to do so once all the legalities have been finalized by the courts.

"What do you want with the cottage?" Jessica asked. She had to admit that was another detail that she hadn't honed in on until that very moment.

"Well, I have been in discussion with the Ryans, and it is my idea to set up a second shop in the cottage."

"Really?" Jessica asked in wonder.

"Yes. I'm quite serious about my plan. To have it a walk from the castle will be ideal for a shop to sell small antiques. Oh, my plan is to also offer service of tea, scones, and the like to guests walking the grounds. Knowing Amy's enjoyment of such treats, I'm sure she would have approved. That's why I'll be moving the portrait there though. With the unfortunate events that surrounded Amy's end, obviously to focus on Evelyn Lansing's story would be more conducive to success than focusing on Amy's."

"Obviously," Alain said before Jessica surreptitiously pinched him.

But Callahan didn't seem to notice.

"I'll have a showcase there, as well, for copies of Evelyn's writings," Callahan said. "The original copies of her writings will go to a historical society, of course. I am a practical man, you see. And who knows? The drama of Evelyn's story might make for good theater. During the summer months, I might also consider a repertory project or two. You may not know this, but during my university days, I dabbled in the dramatic arts. So, by the way, did Dev Matthews, as well as a few of our other former graduates of university. As it happens, we had dinner together recently and were talking about the good old days. I think the recollection of that dinner gave me the idea."

Jessica suddenly had a funny thought while thinking about the likes of Callahan and Matthews in theater costumes. Both men seemed so very different from each other and somehow unlikely to make a success of Callahan's plan. But a light bulb went off in her active brain and she said, "Mr. Callahan, may I have your card? If you do go through with this summer theater idea, I might know just the right woman to help you kick off the project—that is if you like dogs!"

Callahan looked perplexed but said, "Of course." Then he handed Jessica one of his cards from a small holder on a side table. "Now how about I show this young man a beautiful necklace that he may purchase for you to match your lovely bracelet?"

****

Jessica and Alain made it to Dublin by early afternoon. They parked the car and found Beatrice Jones by prior arrangement with the help of Peggy, Louis Aspen's assistant. They were meeting in the same pub in Temple Bar that they had met her in before. This time, Beatrice was wearing a frock and the dress managed to make her look younger than the last time they had all gotten together. Jessica could now appreciate the woman who had been Louis Aspen's muse. Beatrice now looked as she must have when she was a young actress under the spell of her theater producer; she looked almost exactly as she had appeared in the posters that Peggy had showed them in Aspen's office that last time in Dublin.

The first thing that Jessica did was hand over Paul Callahan's card. After much discussion and initial hesitation on Beatrice's part, the former theater actress finally agreed to accept it.

"I promise to at least make contact with your antiques dealer and see what our initial discussion produces," Beatrice said.

"That's all I can ask," Jessica said. The three spent the next hour reviewing the strange and unfortunate events that had unfolded at Castle Ryan and the hopeful new chapter likely ahead for it.

Finally, Beatrice said, "Speaking of production, how did Louis take you both nixing his latest project?" Before Jessica could say anything, Beatrice added, "No. Come to think of it, don't tell me. Let's let sleeping dogs lie. Louis is Michael Thornes's problem now. But if I do connect with this Paul Callahan of yours, Jessica, maybe I can also get him to gallery my doggie paintings. Some of them haven't sold for so long, they might be considered antiques. What do you think?"

"Now that's a plan!" Jessica said, observing one artistic trajectory coming full circle.

Only then, after the actress and Jessica and Alain went their separate ways, did Jessica consider her three stops accomplished. And now it was Alain's turn to guide the car through Dublin and then on through the Irish countryside for a trip, with any luck, without any ghosts to share it with!

Epilogue

In a quiet corner of the Castle Ryan estate, in the center of a small grove of yew trees, is a plot of ground forgotten by many. A small tombstone stands upright, defying the wear and tear of the many years since it was first placed there, defying the winds and the rains of autumn, the snows of winter, and the shining sun of spring and summer.

In this plot, so many years ago, was put to rest the lively, lithe body of Evelyn Lansing. When she first arrived at Castle Ryan and found the spot in her early, happy days, it was her wish that it would be where she would lie in her final resting place so that the soft ground would rest above her head. So despite the few ensuing years with all their unhappiness, and the acrimony that followed, her husband, Bailey, had acquiesced and placed her down in this very spot when it was time to do so.

It was a spot far enough from the castle and from the servants so if from time to time a young man, who would have loved to share her bed and her life so much more so than only publish her stories, came to lay some flowers there, no one was to see. And if he lived always regretting his temerity and failure to appear the night they planned to run away together, and all those hours that Evelyn waited outside in the storm never expecting he would fail to appear, it was his punishment. And he bore it until the day he died and finally joined her.

But Evelyn knew about all those visits to the plot before that final day. And she watched then and now, as she watches all that happens at Castle Ryan and always will. And if one passes the plot and thinks one sees the fleeting image of a sprig of roses the color of blood placed on the soft, brown earth that is covered with tufts of green grass, well, one may be forgiven.

CPSIA information can be obtained
at www.ICGtesting.com
Printed in the USA
BVHW031415130921
616663BV00002B/106/J

9 781665 708968